ALSO BY TERRY TRUEMAN

No Right Turn

BY

TERRY TRUEMAN

🍃 HarperTempest
An Imprint of HarperCollins*Publishers*

Library of Congress Cataloging-in-Publication Data
Trueman, Terry.
  No right turn / by Terry Trueman.— 1st ed.
     p.   cm.
  Summary: After three years of wanting only to be invisible,
sixteen-year-old Jordan begins to recover from his father's
suicide and start living again when a neighbor's vintage
Corvette Stingray opens up new possibilities for him.
  ISBN-10: 0-06-057491-7 (trade bdg.)
  ISBN-13: 978-0-06-057491-8 (trade bdg.)
  ISBN-10: 0-06-057492-5 (lib. bdg.)
  ISBN-13: 978-0-06-057492-5 (lib. bdg.)
  [1. Corvette automobile—Fiction. 2. Automobiles—
Fiction. 3. Grief—Fiction. 4. Suicide—Fiction. 5. Fathers
and sons—Fiction. 6. Washington (State)—Fiction.] I. Title.
PZ7.T7813No 2006   2005005075
[Fic]—dc22   CIP
                                                  AC

Typography by Andrea Vandergrift
5 6 7 8 9 10
❖
First Edition

This one's for
George and Pauly—great, great men,
but bad, bad boys!!
And for my father,
Sydney McDaniel Trueman

THREE YEARS AGO . . .

I heard the gunshot and I knew what had happened. Even before I made it downstairs to Dad's office, I knew what he'd done.

The last time I ever talked to my dad, I didn't know it was going to be the last time, and I've wondered a million times since then if *he* knew.

I'd just gotten home from school; I was thirteen years old. Mom was still at work, and Dad was sitting in his office at our house, moving some papers around on his desk.

"Hey, Jordan," he said.

I answered, "Hi, Dad."

Then, out of the blue, Dad said, "I'm sorry."

I didn't know what he was talking about. I didn't know what to say back.

"What do you mean?" I asked.

"Nothing," Dad said, and kind of smiled.

He took a couple deep slow breaths and then said, in a low, calm voice, "It's all such bullshit."

I've thought about that a hundred times. It's so ironic that my dad, who was always so careful about not swearing in front of me, would leave me with that word; the last word he ever said to me: bullshit. It was only the second time I'd ever heard him say it.

A couple hours after we'd talked, I was in my room and he was still in his office. The shot wasn't that loud, really, just one pop, not even as loud as a big fire-cracker, but I knew instantly what it was, and I ran downstairs.

My father was there in his same chair, at his desk, slumped over, the gun still in his hand.

I could smell the gunpowder, a stink in the air, and see a haze of smoke over the top of Dad, like a little blue cloud.

I ran over to him. His face had a quiet look. I could see where he'd put the gun against his temple and pulled the trigger. There was a little black-and-red hole, small and horrible. I wanted to be sick.

I grabbed the phone on his desk and looked away from him so I could concentrate. I dialed for help.

"Nine-one-one. Please state your emergency."

"My dad shot himself."

"What is your location and who am I speaking to?"

It was like a TV show or a movie. We went back and forth, and it didn't even seem real until I looked at Dad again. "He's not breathing. I want to try CPR."

The lady on the phone said, "That's fine—you go ahead and I'll send help right away. Leave the phone off the hook, and if you need me I'll be right here, okay?"

"Okay," I said.

I set the phone down and stood close to Dad. I honestly don't remember how I managed to get him out of the chair and onto the floor, but I did it. There was a lot of blood, but the bullet hole had stopped bleeding already; I wiped some blood away, but there was no blood on the front of his face or around his mouth.

I hadn't ever had any CPR training, but I'd seen it done on TV before, so I pinched Dad's nose and blew air into his mouth. I just kept blowing over and over again. His chest and belly kept rising and falling. I tried not to think about what I was doing. I tried to pretend that he was going to be all right, but the truth was that he'd shot himself in the head.

I knew my dad was dead, and that what I was doing couldn't save him, but I kept blowing air into his mouth anyway. It was like I was trying to keep him from leaving, even though he was already gone.

It's hard to remember it all now—hard because it was so horrible. I was shaking and crying, trying not to throw up. Not wanting to look at Dad, hating him for what he'd done but wishing I could save him. . . . I don't know. You try to forget something like that, you hate remembering it, but it keeps coming back in nightmares; it keeps coming back other times too; it never really leaves your mind.

It felt like a long time before I finally heard sirens and then a lot longer before the firemen and the cops all came running into our house.

Lots of kids at school didn't have a dad in their lives anymore. That wasn't what you'd call a real exclusive club—but having your old man blow his brains out in the den when he knew you were the only other person in the house—having him not care enough about you to wait until some other time or maybe not even do it at all—well, I wasn't going to find anybody else whose dad hated them enough to do something like that. I know that sounds harsh, but that's how I see it—Dad waited until I was there, all alone with him, then shot himself—great, huh?

I left the football team the week after Dad died. I didn't say anything to the coach or anybody else—I just stopped going to practice, then I quit. I couldn't face my teammates. Football is a game for tough guys, and I'd been a pretty good first-string wide receiver, but I wasn't tough anymore. Somehow, I wasn't . . . anything . . . just a loser with a dead father. I felt embarrassed and humiliated.

"Hey, James." Our team captain, Joey Mender, called to me in the hallway; we always called each other by our last names. I was trying to look invisible, standing at my locker.

I ignored him, and he called to me again as he walked toward me. "Jordan, hey man, what's up?"

I looked at him and shrugged my shoulders.

"Sorry about your dad," he said more softly. "Really, I'm sorry." He hesitated a second and kept standing there. I glanced at him, then away, real quick. What else was there to say? Nothing . . .

Joey finally tried, "The truth is, we could sure use your help against Salk this Friday."

He meant our upcoming game. I spoke softly. "I'm off the team."

"I know. I was just saying—"

I interrupted him. "I'm off. Period."

I slammed my locker and turned my back on him, walking away. Joey was a good guy, but there was nothing left to talk about. There was nothing left to say to anybody. All I wanted was to be alone. What could anybody say to me that would make anything any better? Nothing! What could I say to anybody that would make up for what had happened? Less than nothing.

My mom wanted to help me—she tried to get me to talk to her, but I refused. She had enough to deal with. After all, I'd lost my dad, but she'd lost her husband! There was nothing we could say to each other that would change what had happened, so I didn't see any point in talking about it.

At school I never spoke to anybody unless I had to, and then I always used the fewest words I could manage. It's amazing how easy it is to lose all your friends when you don't return their phone calls and you just ignore them. If you never look anyone in the eyes, if you never speak unless spoken to and then only in the quickest, most uninterested way, the fact is that you *can* become invisible, you *can* eventually be all alone, which was what I wanted.

I actually started to feel that maybe I *was* invisible until one morning when a couple kids from seventh grade walked by me. I didn't even know them, but whenever I had to be around other kids, like in the hallway between classes, I'd go to my locker and stand facing the metal door. At first I'd pretend I was trying to work the combination lock, like maybe I'd forgotten the numbers. But after a while I'd just stand there facing the locker and being real quiet as all the other kids walked behind me, not knowing or caring that I was even there.

"What's with him?" one of the seventh grade guys asked the other kid, kind of whispering.

The second kid answered, not even bothering to lower his voice, "His dad killed himself and he got all messed up."

"How?"

The louder kid laughed. "Whaddya mean, how? Look at him. . . . He's a freakin' zombie!"

They both laughed and kept on walking.

Even though they were just seventh graders, I felt scared to look up at them, ashamed, I guess. I felt my face get red and closed my eyes and tried to take a couple deep breaths. This was exactly what I knew everybody must be thinking: Hey, there's that loser whose old man killed himself. . . . Hey, there's the zombie!

When I finally got the guts to open my eyes and turn slowly around, the hallway was filled with kids rushing past to get to their next classes—nobody was looking at me, nobody cared at all. The longer I stood there and looked at all the kids' faces as they walked by, the more invisible I felt.

Yep, I felt totally alone. But that was what I wanted.

NOW, THREE YEARS LATER . . .

I walk into the house after school and drop my junk by the door and start moving toward the kitchen.

"Hi, sweetie," I hear from the hallway that leads back to the bedrooms.

I about jump out of my skin.

"Mom, what are you doing home?" My mom's a swing-shift nurse at St. Thomas Hospital, two in the afternoon till midnight, Monday through Thursday; she's *never* home at this time of day.

She laughs, walking into the hallway from her bedroom. "Well, it's nice to see you, too."

I say, "I'm just surprised you're here—of course, now I'll have to tell all the guys on the way over with the babes and drugs that the rave is off for today, but, you know, it's your house, too. . . ."

"Babes and drugs, huh?" Mom laughs. "Good, at

least you're not wasting your time on any foolishness like studying."

"Yeah," I agree, "you got that right."

Mom punches me in the arm pretty hard—she's got a good straight right.

In the three years since Dad died, things have just barely started to become normal . . . not *normal*, really. A better word would be "predictable." And we're doing okay—I guess we're kind of getting used to our lives. I didn't think that would ever happen again.

Mom follows me through the living room and into the kitchen.

She asks, "So how was school?"

I shrug, but I catch something strange in the sound of her voice. We've gotten to know each other pretty well these past three years—after all, she's almost the only person I ever talk to—so I can tell that something is up with her. I decide to just wait her out.

It doesn't take long.

"You know Don Lugar?" she asks.

"Who?"

"Mr. Lugar, the man who bought the Andersons' house?"

Now I know. I get a weird feeling; the hair on the

back of my neck stands up. "What about him?" I try not to sound as creeped out or look as uncomfortable as I really feel.

Apparently hiding my feelings works, because Mom says, "Well, he's asked me to go out to a movie this Friday."

She waits for me to say something. I'm shocked, really, and I can't think of anything at all. I draw a total blank, so I stupidly mutter, "What movie?"

She kind of smiles and says, "We're not sure yet—we're going to discuss it."

I think to myself, *We're,* huh? You and your new boyfriend? I also think, You couldn't keep your last husband alive. What makes you sure you'll do any better this time? Even as I think this, I know it's unfair—maybe not totally unfair, but at least pretty shitty.

Mom, not smiling now, her voice kind of soft and serious, asks, "Are you okay with that?"

"Yeah," I lie.

Mom looks into my eyes and asks, "Are you sure?"

"Yeah," I say again, kind of impatiently. What's she want from me—a seal of approval?

The fact is that it wasn't Mom who was here when Dad killed himself; it wasn't Mom who had to deal with that. Nope. Dad made sure that was a special treat, just for me!

It's Friday night, and I'm trying not to stare out the front window of our house. Don Lugar was supposed to be here at six o'clock to pick Mom up, and it's already six oh three, so I'm feeling kind of good that he's late, when suddenly I see, down the street where he lives, his classic Corvette Stingray backing out of his driveway and cruising slowly up Northridge Road to our house.

I stand back a little, out of sight. Once he stops in our driveway, he climbs out of the 'Vette and walks up to our front door.

He rings the doorbell and Mom hollers down to me from her bedroom, "Jordan, will you get the door, please?"

What am I, the butler? I quietly duck down the hallway and into my room, pretending I didn't hear her.

The doorbell rings again, and I hear Mom hurry out of her room and down the hall.

She opens the door and says, "Hi." I can actually hear the smile in her voice.

Don Lugar says, "Hi," then, "Sorry I'm late."

I glance at my watch. Late? It's only five minutes

after six. What a dork!

They speak quietly for a moment or two, and then I hear them both laugh. From my bedroom I glance out the window at the Corvette.

"Jordan!" I hear Mom call me.

I don't answer; then I hear her walking toward me. "Jordan!" she calls again, louder.

There's no escaping. "Yeah," I answer.

Mom says, "Come here, please."

I walk out of my bedroom and down the hallway. It's greet-the-new-boyfriend time—great!

"Honey," Mom says, "I'd like you to meet Don Lugar."

He's standing there looking at me. By his expression I'm guessing that he's as uncomfortable as I am.

"Hey," I say, offering my hand.

"Nice to meet you, Jordan," he says, shaking my hand firmly. "Your mom's told me quite a bit about you."

I almost burst out laughing. What could she have told him? There's absolutely nothing to tell. I'd like to blurt out an imitation of what Mom must have said: "My son is a freakin' zombie: no friends, no interests, no *life*, you're gonna love him!"

But instead I just say, "Nice to meet you, too."

There's an awkward pause. Just to break the silence

I say, "Nice 'Vette."

Don smiles and says, "Thanks."

Mom smiles too.

I try to smile, but it's pretty phony—this whole scene is just so weird. Don says, "Drop by sometime and I'll show you the car, take you for a ride."

I say *to myself*, Are you trying a little too hard, mister? But I say *out loud*, "Sure, that'd be cool."

It'll be a cold day in hell before I'd go hang out with Mom's new little pal. It may be I'm pathetic, I *am* pathetic, but I refuse to believe that I'm *that* pathetic. . . .

We hem and haw for another few uncomfortable moments. I notice that Mom looks really nice. She's wearing a black silk blouse tucked into her tight black jeans. She has on boots with tall heels, giving her an extra couple inches. Her makeup in the light of the hallway makes her look young, and most of all, she has a perma-grin. She's really happy. I haven't seen her smile like this in a long time.

I have mixed feelings. I'm glad for her in one way—it's good to see her so excited—but it's like I don't know why she gets to go out and be happy all of a sudden. I mean, just like that, her life is back to normal? I'm being a jerk, I know, but I don't get any of this.

Finally Don says to me, "Well, we won't be late." Like he's checking in with me for permission and like I'm the parent.

I don't know what else to say, so I speak in a deep voice. "All right, you kids have a good time now, but drive carefully."

It's kind of a lame joke, and they both laugh way too hard.

It's a relief when they finally walk out the door. The second they're gone, I race back down the hallway to my bedroom and peek out just in time to see Don open the passenger door and Mom, kind of awkwardly, slip into the car. Then Don walks around to the driver's side and hops in too. The car's windows are tinted dark, and I can't see in very well. He fires up the engine; it has a pretty decent roar. They back out and take off.

I decide right away that he's an idiot and that I'm not going to like him. Period.

Cool car, though.

ONE

I'm walking home from school after getting off the bus. It's the following Tuesday, and I go past Don Lugar's house. In his driveway he's polishing the Stingray. I've never been a gearhead, never cared that much about cars. It's not like Mom and I have had thousands of extra bucks to burn on anything. So cars have never been that big a deal to me, and big-boy toys like Corvette Stingrays are about as realistic to me as . . . I don't know . . . as nothing, they're just something I know I'll never have.

My dad had always talked and acted like he *hated* muscle cars and cool classics—he called them "show-off cars." Whenever we saw one on the road, he'd always say something about "what a waste of money" or he'd look at the driver, usually some middle-aged guy like himself, and mutter, "Grow up."

But there's something about my dad that's bugged me ever since he died. On the day of Dad's funeral, afterward, everybody came back to our house to sit around and drink punch and eat cookies and try and pretend that everything was going to be okay. I couldn't stand it, so I left the living room, where a lot of people were sitting and standing around. The kitchen was just as crowded. I didn't know where to hide until I spotted the closed door to Dad's office. I didn't want to go back in there, I really didn't, but I knew that it would give me some privacy. And truthfully, something weird pounded in my head—a strange feeling of being pulled toward that closed door and then on into the room. So that's where I went.

It was already all cleaned up; some of Mom's friends from the hospital, other nurses, had taken care of it. I took a slow breath and started looking around. Pretty soon I started snooping through Dad's stuff.

Most of the things I'd seen a million times. But in the bottom drawer of his big oak desk, hidden under a pile of old bills and manila folders, and I mean really hidden, like it was a secret porno stash, I found a stack of magazines and books. I looked at the dates on them and they went back for years. There were dozens of them: hot-rod magazines, boating magazines, hang gliding, flying, and skydiving, all these magazines and books that I'd never seen before. One of the books was called *Sports Car Color History, Corvette 1968–1982*.

Why did my dad have all this crap? Why did he hide it? What good was any of this to him since he'd never skydived, hang glided, owned a boat or a hot rod? And if my dad had hated 'Vettes so much, like he always sounded when we saw one, why did he have a book about them? I glanced at the magazines and thumbed through a few of the books, but I didn't stay in there very long; the room gave me the creeps. I put everything back where I'd found it and got out.

So when Don Lugar showed up at our house driving his Corvette, I wondered what Dad would have thought about it. What would Dad have thought about a guy who actually had a *real* show-off car, hitting on Mom?

Don's taller than my dad was; he dresses just like most older guys—kind of dorky. Now he looks up and says, "Hi, Jordan, how you doin'?" like we're already old pals or something.

"Not bad." I pause, I want to just keep walking, I want to ignore Don, but I can't stop staring at his car.

I haven't ever had a chance to really look at a Corvette up close before.

I ask, "What year?"

Don says, "It's a 1976."

1970s Stingrays have that long, sleek Coke bottle shape—high curved fenders over the wheels, low to the ground. Don's has what looks like a custom paint job, white on top and a teal blue-green all along the lower section.

Almost against my will, I walk over to where Don wipes a soft cloth over the shiny hood. The closer I get, the prettier the car is. The white upper body is metallic, kind of cream colored with little flecks of silver in it. The windows are tinted dark, smoky gray, almost black. The tires are big, wider than the tires on normal cars, and there are bright chrome hubs.

I blurt out, "Man . . ." but then shut up, managing not to suck up too much.

I mean, I could care less whether Don likes me or not, in fact I hope he *doesn't*—I'm just having this weird reaction to the car.

He smiles. Don moved into our neighborhood about a year ago, bought the Andersons' house on the east side of Northridge Road—the view side. It's a large, family-type home, but he lives there alone and keeps to himself. I had spoken to Don maybe two or three minutes in the whole year he's lived three houses away from ours, right up to the day he came to pick up Mom for their date. Truthfully, I wouldn't say more than "hi" right now if it weren't for the Corvette.

But the car is *so* beautiful, *so* sleek and powerful looking that it seems to call me over to it. All those times my dad put down cool cars, I'd never thought much about it—until now. Realizing I'm being kind of rude, I hesitate before staring into the windows, which are tinted too dark for me to see inside anyway—rude or not, I can't stop myself. I've gotta see more.

Don says, "Open the door if you want to take a look."

I don't even answer; I just swing the heavy door open. The interior is outlaw black.

"Cool," I say softly, talking to myself.

Don laughs. "Yeah, she's my baby."

"Is it as fast as it looks?"

Don says, "She was built back when there were more stringent emission controls, so she's no monster. But compared to everything else built in '76, she could hold her own. Plus I'm doing some tweaking here and there, juicing her up. So, yeah, she's plenty fast."

"Yeah," I say, not really understanding what he's talking about.

"You wanna go for a spin?" he asks.

Like I mentioned before, I've been pretty much out of it since my dad died. What's Don thinking? That he can win me over just by taking me for a ride?

I look at the car again and can't stop myself from asking, "Really?" I feel weird.

Don smiles again. "Every guy in the world who buys a 'Vette is dying to show her off."

I ask, "Where?"

"Just a quick run up onto the prairie. I'll show you what she can do."

My dad would have disapproved, would have warned me against taking such a chance. Dad never took a chance in his life, *ever*! Then again, what good did that do him?

Before I know I'm going to say it, I hear words flying out of my mouth, "Sure, let's go."

I glance at his license plate:

I wonder, Who the hell is Nos?

I shouldn't be doing this, I think as I climb into the Corvette and buckle up. If Don Lugar thinks he can buy me off this easy, he's dumber than he looks.

But what the hell.

TWO

He fires the engine, and a soft rumble, deep and powerful, vibrates through my whole body. I've never heard or felt anything like it before.

We back out of the driveway.

As we move forward, it's like we're bumping over the surface. This car is nothing like my mom's Honda or any of the other newer rigs in which I've ever ridden. Riding in the Stingray is like being strapped onto the back of an animal, maybe an oversized cheetah. It feels like the car has a mind of its own. *It's* taking *us* for a ride, not the other way around.

We reach the stop sign at the end of our street.

"You ready?" Don asks.

I'm not sure what he means, but I answer, "Sure."

Don cranks it through the turn, and then he punches it.

The jolt is unlike any rush I've ever felt before. The

car shoots forward, and the back of my head slams against the tall bucket seat. A roar replaces the soft animal rumble.

I glance at the speedometer and notice that it isn't working, but in only a few seconds we're flying. I grab the black vinyl handle on the door. A hundred yards ahead is a sharp curve, a ninety-degree turn to the left where Cedar Road turns into Strong Road. As we get closer to it, I squeeze the door grip even harder.

Don barely eases off the gas as the 'Vette screams into the turn.

Everything moves incredibly fast. In half a second we're through the curve and pounding along the straight stretch ahead of us.

I start to ease my hold on the door grip when Don guns it again. In a few seconds we're going really fast. The rush is incredible: the rumble of the engine, the deep vibration of the car, the way that every bump and dip in the road registers through my feet and legs and ass.

Trying not to sound too scared, I say, "We must be going a hundred."

Don glances down at the tachometer on the dashboard and says, "Oops . . . more like a hundred and ten."

He immediately backs off the gas and smiles over

at me. "Sorry about that. . . . She kinda likes to go."

I say, "No, this is great."

As the 'Vette slows down, he asks, "Is she fast enough for you?"

I laugh and answer sarcastically, "I guess."

Don laughs too. "You like it?"

I don't hesitate. "I love it." Then I ask, "Is your speedometer broken?"

Don says, "Yeah, I'm waiting on a part for it, a new head. But you can tell your speed by the tach. Every line mark on the tach is a hundred rpms, which equals five miles per hour . . . a thousand rpms is fifty miles per hour, fifteen hundred rpms is seventy-five miles per hour, and so on."

"And we were going a hundred and ten?"

"Yep, pretty close to that."

Unable to stop myself, I ask, "Did you drive like this when my mom was with you?"

Don laughs out loud. "Shit no!"

I laugh too.

We cruise on for a ways at a more sane speed, not even talking. Although only five miles north of Spokane, the prairie is mostly fields and pastures and old farmhouses, horses, a few cows. It feels like we've gone backward in time. I wonder if my dad, who grew up a few miles from this same neighborhood on

Spokane's north side, ever flew down Strong Road at 110 mph. I can't *imagine* it.

Don suddenly asks, "You wanna drive her?"

I feel a jolt of adrenaline. "Me? Drive? I've never driven a car like this."

Don, I think teasing me, says, "No kidding? Well, there's always a first time. You drive your mom's Honda, right?"

"Yeah," I answer, not mentioning that Mom's Honda has *nothing* to do with this Stingray—they're not just different machines from different times, they're in different universes.

A few seconds later Don pulls over to the side of the road, onto the dirt parking strip. There are no other cars in sight.

A rush of crummy thoughts races through my head again. Why would this guy let me drive his cool car? What's he want from me? These thoughts aren't in my dad's voice, but they might as well be. Does Don think that he's going to take my dad's place? The last thing I need is another dad—the last thing I need is to go through something like that again. . . .

I try to push these thoughts away as we trade seats and I grip the steering wheel.

Don says, "When you feel comfortable, just slip

the gearshift into drive, the top D, and ease the accelerator down. We don't want to throw any gravel—this *is* a fiberglass body."

I pause, trying to get comfortable. After a few seconds, finally, I put the shifter into drive. My foot still on the brake, I'm surprised how cool and calm I feel. I check both directions. The coast is clear, and I ease out onto Strong Road.

My dad would *not* approve!

Of course, that makes this even better.

Back in Don's driveway, I get out of the car and close the door behind me. Don climbs out too.

I look over at him. "That was pretty incredible. Thanks."

"My pleasure."

For some reason I don't like the sound of him saying the word "pleasure." It's stupid of me, I know he's just being polite; still, something about it feels weird. Pleasure . . . Mom . . . yuck!

But something else bothers me even more, something I hope Don can't see in my face. As I look back at the Stingray, studying the car's long, sleek body, I know I *have to* drive it again—I've *gotta* feel that rush I felt going over a hundred miles an hour, even though

I know that Don would never let me drive it that fast.

"I'll see you, Don," I say. "And thanks again for the ride. It's a great car."

He smiles, "You're welcome. Come by anytime."

As I reach the street, I yell back to him, "By the way, the keys are in it."

Don, maybe absentmindedly, maybe just distracted, answers, "I park her in the garage, so I always leave the keys in her in case of a fire or something—she'd be the first thing I'd save."

I think, The keys are always in her, huh? Is that right?

Maybe there *is* a way I can go 110 again—maybe there's a way I can drive that fast all by myself!

THREE

When Mom gets home from work, the first thing she asks is what she always asks: "How was school?"

Of course, school's an ancient memory—I'm still thinking about Corvette Stingrays, about going 110 mph on the prairie. Mentioning that little detail, the 110 mph thing, doesn't seem like the best way to start this conversation. Still, I have to say something about it.

"I saw Don Lugar. He was out working on his 'Vette."

"That's nice," Mom says, pretending that she isn't paying much attention.

"I mean, it's the most beautiful car I've ever seen."

Mom glances over at me and laughs. "I *know*," she says, all excited. "It *is* fun, isn't it?" She pauses and smiles again and puts her hand up against my face. "You don't think you're getting a Corvette anytime real soon, do you, honey? I mean, when you're older, you can—"

I interrupt, laughing, "Yeah, right! But he gave me a ride in it."

Mom asks, "He gave you a ride? In the 'Vette? Really?"

She sounds so silly. I had hoped her reaction would be more like mine—kind of a mix of suspicion and criticism—at least a little bit annoyed that Don was trying too hard to impress me. Instead she sounds so flippin' happy.

I hate how she asked, "*In the 'Vette?*" Like she's all into the lingo now?

I'm not too surprised, though. Frankly, Dad always had the "common sense" in our family—Mom always had more fun.

I say, "We just cruised up to the prairie, a short ride, ten minutes or so. He said he wanted to show me what the car was like. We went for a quick spin."

Mom, sounding slightly more sane again, asks, "Did you like it?"

I admit, "Oh, yeah. It was wayyy cool."

"And Don didn't mind showing it to you?" She's still obviously happy. I'm getting more and more annoyed.

I just say, "No."

Mom says, "Well, that's nice. I'm glad you had fun, honey; I'm glad you and Don are getting to know each other. And if he wanted to show you the car, I guess there's no harm done." She hesitates a second and then says, "I'm glad to see you excited about something. . . ." She stops herself from saying more, but I know what she's thinking; she's relieved to see me enjoying *any-thing* at all.

I think about my insane need to get behind the wheel of the 'Vette again.

I think about Mom's words: "No harm done."

I smile to myself.

FOUR

If I had to name my closest friend at school, where I don't actually have *any* close friends, I'd say it's Wally Britton. I think this is because he's, maybe, almost as much of a social misfit as me. He has funky red hair, real wavy, like curly fries soaked in ketchup, and he's kind of skinny and wears old hippie-frame glasses when he doesn't have his contacts in. He carries a cell phone in a little leather case, clipped to his belt, and I've never, not once, *ever* seen him use it. For all I know it could be fake.

When my dad died and I was in middle school, like I mentioned, I got rid of all my friends, but I met Wally at the start of high school. He'd gone to a different middle school than me, and when I told him that my dad had died (not *how* he'd died, just that he was dead) and that I didn't like to talk about it, Wally said that was cool—he didn't want to talk about it either.

You could say that Wally is empathy impaired. Still, being as out of it as I've been for these last three years, it's useful to know someone who still circulates on the edge of the real world.

I call Wally and tell him about riding in Don's 'Vette.

"He's the guy who's trying to get into yer mom's pants, isn't he?" Wally asks.

Great minds think alike (then again, so do moronic, perverted ones).

I answer, "Yeah, I guess. I don't know what he wants. What I *do* know is that I'm gonna drive the Corvette again."

"What do you mean?" Wally asks. "Is this Don guy into some kind of Big Brothers trip with you now? Aren't you a little old for that?" He laughs.

I say, "No, Wally. Do I have to spell it out for you? I'm gonna find some way to drive that car again—even if I have to sneak it out."

"Sneak it out," Wally says with a real sarcastic tone. "You mean steal it. Good plan," he adds, even more sarcastically. "Do you know what days are reserved for prison visitations?"

Sometimes Wally can be pretty annoying.

* * *

Two weeks later, to the day, I'm ready to steal Don Lugar's Corvette.

Wally's right; that's what it is, grand theft auto. I don't care.

I tell myself that sneaking the car out for a joyride isn't *really* stealing, since I plan to bring it back. Of course, if I get caught, who'll believe me? I tell myself that stealing it is partly Don's own fault, for letting me drive such an incredible car in the first place (how's a guy supposed to drive a Honda after that?) and for interfering with Mom's and my fragile, crappy lives. Plus, why should Mom get to move on when I don't even have a life? I know this is mostly bull, but it's what I feel. So Don isn't innocent in this—that's what I tell myself.

There's something else, too, though—something bigger than all these other excuses. The truth is that going 110 mph that day on the prairie was the first time since Dad died where I did *not* feel like . . . well . . . like some kind of zombie.

After that ride in Don's 'Vette, after I drove the car, whenever I get home from school, and he's out cleaning or tinkering with it, I always stop by and we b.s. I ask about the car, but not too much; I don't want him to get suspicious. Mostly we talk about nothing: the weather, neighborhood gossip, nothing important. He never asks anything personal about me, and I don't ask about him either. We don't talk about my mom too much, even though they've gone out a few more times—movies, dinners, rides in his car. The only personal thing he's mentioned is that he was divorced years ago, before he moved into our neighborhood.

If Don knows about my dad dying, and he must know something just by knowing Mom, he's never said anything about it to me. The more time we spend together, the more he seems to relax. He swears a lot, not like an old guy wanting to show me how hip he is, more like he just always talks that way. He's funny and smart, my dad's age, but *totally* different from Dad. I'm starting to think of Don, a little bit, like he's kind of a friend, not a *real* friend, of course, I mean the guy's like fifty or something, but kind of a friend—yeah, right, a friend whose car I'm going to rip off.

Knowing all along that I have to drive the 'Vette again, I've planned how to do it. Don works in insurance, sells it, I think. He goes to appointments most days, and *every* Wednesday night he is out of town for the whole night, working with his customers in Wenatchee, 150 miles away.

I watched him punch in the code to his garage

door, seeing the numbers—53773—so I can get into where he parks the 'Vette. He has a double-car garage and his other car is an almost-new Pontiac, his daily driver and his "work car." So he's gone, every Wednesday night, and the 'Vette's just sitting there.

Mom works late too. Before Dad died, he and I would be home together, but now, Monday through Thursday, I'm always home alone. Mom usually gets back a little after midnight.

My school nights are always the same. I eat some dinner, then watch TV or listen to music or play video games. If absolutely all else fails, maybe I'll finally do a little homework. I try not to think about my dad and all the crap he used to say to me: "Strike while the iron's hot," "A bird in the hand is worth two in the bush," "Safety first." He'd been a true master of clichés and worthless advice. And at the end what did he leave me with? "Bullshit." Great, Dad, big help! So just how boring is my life? Totally and completely. And what, exactly, do I stand to lose by stealing Don Lugar's Corvette? Not much. Maybe my dad always dreamed of doing wild stuff, taking risks, having fun. Maybe Dad dreamed about it, but he never did anything!

I don't want to be him!

I'm not him!

* * *

So it's Wednesday night. I dress in dark clothes and walk quietly from my house over to Don's place. From looking around at his garage during earlier visits, I know that there's lots of junk—not junk, but *stuff* all over the place: an expensive ten-speed bike hanging from hooks in the ceiling; some sports gear, like basketballs and volleyballs in a mesh bag; a workbench crowded with tools. I've made mental notes about the layout of the place so that I can move around in the dark. On the right side of the two-car garage is the Stingray.

The only light in Don's driveway comes from a streetlight. I don't want to draw the attention of any neighbors by turning on the garage light once I get inside, but this plan is instantly messed up. When I punch in the code and the garage door goes up, a light automatically comes on too. I'm standing here like an idiot, basking in what feels like about ten billion watts; I hurry into the garage and hide myself against the wall.

After a few minutes the light finally goes off. It's dark again. Even though the night is kind of cold, I'm sweating like crazy. I find the door handle of the car and quietly open it. Instantly, the scent of the car—leather and cleaning polish and air freshener—remind me of my first ride, and I calm down.

I know that once I start the car, I'll be past the

point of no return—who am I kidding? I've already broken into this guy's garage, so that's breaking and entering. Now I'm going to take his car out without his permission. Like I said, grand theft auto.

I take another slow, deep breath and reach down on the steering column and find the keys. At least I'm smart enough not to start the car and let it run inside the garage, where I'd get killed by carbon monoxide.

"Smart?" I can hear my dad's voice playing in my head. "Do you really think that *anything* you're doing shows any intelligence? Are you nuts? What are you trying to prove?"

"Up yours, Dad, you're not even alive," I say softly to myself. "And I'm not doing this to *prove* anything— I'm just *doing* it."

A few more deep breaths and I turn the ignition key. The car starts instantly. I sit frozen, waiting for the FBI or SWAT or somebody to blow me away. But there's nothing—just the loud purr of the 'Vette as it echoes out of the garage into the darkness.

I back out and, as soon as I'm clear, push the button on the remote control hanging on the sun visor to close the garage door.

In the street I leave the headlights off and try to will myself to be invisible. I super-gently slip the car into drive, like if I shift quietly enough, no one will look out and realize that Don Lugar's beautiful Corvette Stingray is moving up our street with no headlights on.

I drive the long block up Northridge Road as the engine rumbles. At the stop sign I pull on the head-lights and glance at the dash, noticing that my high beams are on. I try to find the lever on the steering col-umn to dim them. Nothing works until I realize that the dimmer switch is on the floor of the car, under my left foot.

Pulling out onto Cedar Road, I head south, down the hill, afraid to try to negotiate the sharp right turn that Don made that day of our ride. I barely touch the gas; the steepness of the hill pulls me along. Cedar winds around in sharp curves, a fun place for going fast if it weren't for the deer that sometimes jump into the road from the trees and heavy brush growing there.

At the bottom of Cedar I stop at the stop sign and find myself in the left-hand turn lane. The only traffic on the road, the *only* other car within sight at the inter-section at this exact moment, is a green-and-white county sheriff's car waiting on my right to turn onto Cedar.

I freeze. Everything I'm doing rushes through my

brain. My heart pounds wildly; my palms become instantly sweaty; for half a second I actually think I might piss my pants, throw up, or faint, all at the same moment. How could this happen? I haven't seen a single other car since I left Don's driveway, not *one*! But here's a sheriff.

I stare straight ahead.

He turns slowly, agonizingly slowly, right in front of me and rolls by, heading up Cedar Road toward the prairie.

With no other traffic in sight, and sitting here in the left-turn lane, I have to go, so I ease away from the stop sign and slowly accelerate down Country Homes Boulevard. The 'Vette rumbles softly. I glance up to my left and see the flickering of the cop's headlights as he moves past the trees and away from me. God, I feel great!

Not wanting to push my luck, I just make a quick loop, going only a few miles down Country Homes to Wall, where I take a left and then up Five Mile Road, a long winding hill that leads back up to the prairie. Because both Cedar Road and Five Mile Road go to the same place, and that cop just went up Cedar only a few minutes ago, I take it real easy, obeying the speed limit except for one short stretch, a hundred yards of sharp curves, where I give the 'Vette a little more juice.

Don has fixed the speedometer. I jump from thirty-five to sixty in about two seconds. After gliding through the sharp turns, I back off the gas again and take it slow the rest of the way. I notice that I'm breathing really hard. My heart is beating about ten million times per minute.

Before I know it, I'm turning back onto Northridge Road again. All told, I've been out in the car for only ten minutes, fifteen at the most. I ease back toward Don's driveway. As I get closer, I get scared again. What if Don came home unexpectedly? He could be calling the cops at this very second! What if my mom is home, too, and somehow knows that I'm out committing all these felonies?

But when I reach Don's driveway, his house is dark.

I hit the garage door opener, and I pull the Corvette in, easing slowly forward.

I turn off the ignition and double-check everything—the position of the seat; the little sliding cover over the ashtray and cigarette lighter that I noticed flew open when I gunned it; the headlights, making sure the bug eyes have closed properly. As anxious as I am to get out of here, I force myself to stay calm, not wanting to screw up. Once everything looks right, I climb out of the car.

As I walk away, I glance back one more time at the

'Vette. I know I'm crazy to think it, but I can almost feel the car smiling at me, can almost hear it whispering, "Until next time."

I think to myself, and even say out loud, "No way."

But then I get back home and walk through the door and yell, "Mom!" and get no answer. I go up to my bedroom and look out at Don's house, so quiet in the dark, the garage door closed, everything so still and normal. I look around my room and see the framed picture of my dad on my chest of drawers. He's looking back at me in the only way that I can remember him *ever* looking now—that is, disapproving. But I think, So what, he's dead: All his rules, all his "wise" sayings are meaningless; he's nothing anymore. I stare at Dad's face in the picture and feel a familiar feeling rising up in me again—a weird kind of numbness. But I also feel something else, too, something I haven't really felt for a long time—anger.

What would you think of what I've just done, Dad?

What would you say?

Ask somebody who gives a damn!

And now I know that the 'Vette is right. . . .

I'll be back.

FIVE

At school the next day I tell Wally what I've done.

"You're nuts!" he says. Then, "How was it?"

I admit, "Totally incredible."

Wally asks, "What if you'd gotten caught?"

"I didn't, though."

"Yeah, but what if you had?"

"I didn't."

"Yeah, but—"

I interrupt. "I was careful, Wal."

He shakes his head, laughing, and mutters, "Is that why you almost ran into a cop?"

"I didn't 'almost run into' anybody. I saw a cop, that's all."

"You're an idiot."

I laugh at this, and Wally gets a weird expression on his face.

"What?" I ask.

"What was that sound you just made?"

I ask, "What do you mean?"

Wally says, "Was that a laugh? Did you actually just laugh then? I've known you for two years now and I've never heard you laugh before. . . . I've never even seen you *smile*!"

"Up yours," I say, laughing again, but I have to admit he has a point.

A few days later, when I get off the bus from school, Don's out working on the Corvette in his driveway. I hope he won't say anything to me. I'm nervous that somehow he knows what I've done.

"Hey, Jordan," he calls out.

Damn. Concerned, but trying not to show it, I force myself to look up at him, smile, and say, "Hi, Don."

He looks okay, not suspicious or mad, just normal.

"How you doin'?" he asks.

"Great," I answer, and walk over to him.

Suddenly I have this weird feeling, something different from just nerves, kind of a sick, guilty thing. Standing next to Don reminds me of one time in eighth grade, just a few months before Dad died. My best friend back then had been Will Nicholson, and he had a crush on Patti Martin. Will talked about her *all* the time. I listened and pretended that I cared. One day, when Will wasn't around, Patti asked *me* if I'd take her to the school dance that Friday. She kind of stared at her shoes part of the time and into my eyes the rest. I could tell she liked me. Of course, I told her no; after all, she was Will's girlfriend whether she knew it or not. I avoided her for several days, after which she started going out with Alan Mender, breaking Will's heart (it took Will several hours to fall in love with Suzie Spangle). Anyway, standing next to Don and his car, I feel the same way I felt when I first saw Will after Patti asked me to the dance; guilty and bad, trapped by an unwanted secret.

Don has the hood up on the 'Vette, and for the first time I see the engine.

"Wow," I say, staring at it shining in the sunlight. The glare off the chrome is almost blinding. "Is that . . . normal? I mean, are all Corvettes' motors like that?"

Don laughs. "No. The chrome is all custom: K&N air filter and Edelbrock valve covers. This plate here"— he points at a flat chrome piece at the back of the engine compartment—"I had to order this from over on the coast; it's an ignition shield."

Some of the wires and all the hoses are covered in a shiny metal material, like tape, only thicker. I ask, "What are these for?"

"Just for looks. I'm getting her ready to show at

some little country Show and Shines—just for fun."

"Cool," I say.

Don keeps working on the engine of his car, cleaning the chrome with a soft cloth so that it shines even brighter than before.

For some reason I think about my dad again. I guess since Don is hanging out with Mom, it's only natural that I'm kind of comparing him to Dad, but they seem so different from each other. Dad went to work and he read the paper and he liked to watch sports, especially baseball and college football. Dad was always just . . . I don't know how to describe it . . . kind of quiet and . . . I guess *restrained* is a good word. He always tried to avoid problems—I don't think he ever even yelled at me.

Don looks up and interrupts my thoughts. "Grab that rag, Jordan."

"What?" I ask.

"If you're gonna hang out, you might as well learn how to treat a lady right."

I smile. This is the kind of thing Don says sometimes—the kind of thing Dad would never have said.

SIX

It's useless trying to hide my obsession about the Stingray from Don.

On the third day in a row that I stop by, he hands me a soft cotton cloth again and shows me how to polish the chrome wheels and clean the black sidewalls and the white lettering on the oversized tires: BF GOODRICH, T/A RADIAL.

Don says, "When you show a car, it has to look perfect."

"Like this one," I answer.

He laughs. "No, we've got a ways to go before she'll be ready. Some guys in the bigger shows spend hundreds of hours and thousands of dollars on their cars. I don't have that kind of interest or time, but I don't want to embarrass myself." He pauses and pats the front fender of the 'Vette, "I don't want to embarrass her either."

For some reason I think again about that thing with Patti and Will and me. I guess stealing Don's car is kind of like how I'd have felt back then if I'd actually gone to that dance with Patti. Back then I'd have *never* done something like that. Back then, before my dad died, I used to believe that if I did the right thing or at least tried to be good, nothing too bad would happen to me. I used to believe that life was fair. I learned different. Right now I don't care what-all I *used to* believe. Right now all I care about is what I know I'm going to do!

I'm gonna take the car again—and that's that!

Don's bought new tires, new carpeting, and new Corvette floor mats. He's let me help him put even more chrome on the engine. We put on a new alternator and water pump, both of them chrome, and he had the old intake manifold replaced with a new, special one from Edelbrock.

But he's also installed a gray tank that takes up almost all of the tiny cargo space behind the seats.

"What's this?" I ask him, staring at the tank set in steel brackets. It looks kind of like a scuba diver's air tank.

Don smiles and says, "That's the latest improvement to this nasty girl. It's a nitrous oxide system—NOS."

I ask, "So what's it do?" Sometimes I have to remind him that I'm not yet the same level of gearhead that he's becoming.

"See this?" he says, pointing to a red switch on the center console. I nod. Don flips up the red switch, and underneath is another switch, a small silver one.

I joke, "Ejection seat?"

Don smiles. "Kind of. See this?" He reaches back and touches the silver knob on the top of the gray tank.

I nod again.

He explains, "This handle turns on the nitrous. Then, when you flip on this"—he touches the silver switch under the red protective one—"then push the gas pedal to the floor, that kicks the nitrous in."

"And what's that do?"

"It gives you two hundred extra horses."

I try to think what the 'Vette would feel like with that much extra power. It's almost unimaginable.

Almost. But I can imagine real good.

I stare at the gray tank, remembering the procedure Don's just explained; two hundred extra horses.

I mutter, "Two hundred, that's a lot."

"Oh, yeah," Don says. "That's a shitload! And, of course, we're talking about nitrous, a potentially explosive gas—so if something goes wrong at the wrong time, you can pretty quickly become a three-hundred-eighty-horsepower, hundred-fifty-mile-per-hour fireball flying into a million fiberglass pieces and human body parts."

I don't say anything. What's there to say to that? But it's sure something to think about!

SEVEN

The next time I'm ready to go over and steal Don's car again, I phone Wally first.

"Don't do it," Wally says. "I've got a bad feeling."

I laugh. "You always have a bad feeling."

"No," Wally insists. "Really, man, this time it's for real. I mean, think about it—what can make such a stupid risk worthwhile?"

"It's worth it," I say.

"You're a moron," Wally says, and hangs up the phone.

It's Wednesday again; Don is out of town until tomorrow afternoon. No rain or even any serious clouds, just a tiny sliver of new moon.

Getting the car away from the house is much less stressful the second time. Thoughts of arrest, conviction, embarrassment, and totally screwing over Don barely enter my mind as I clear the car out of the garage again and head down Cedar Road.

Although I don't have a real clear plan yet, I want to go for a longer ride than before. I promise myself that I'll leave the nitrous alone. Stupid as I might sometimes be, the idea of turning into a human fireball doesn't sound like much fun.

At the bottom of Cedar Road I go right onto Country Homes Boulevard heading south, toward downtown Spokane. Country Homes is a well-lit street. What's the point of driving a car as beautiful as the 'Vette if nobody sees you doing it? After a block or so, the road changes into Maple, a major one-way arterial. At the first stoplight on Maple I look over at the car on my right, hoping I'll catch somebody admiring the 'Vette, but in that lane are a middle-aged guy and his wife in an older Buick. They don't even notice me.

At the next light, though, only a block ahead, the car in the right lane is a late-model Honda Accord, maybe two or three years old, a decent little rig, clean and with some trick stuff: eighteen-inch chrome wheels, nice paint, and a big HONDA decal running the full length of the back window.

There are four teenaged guys in the car. I can feel

the vibration and hear their bass from their subwoofer. They can't see me through the tinted windows of the 'Vette, but they're all staring at the car, the guys on the passenger sides, front and back, leaning over to get a better look.

We're the first two cars at the light, and when it turns green, we both move forward. After a few yards, about halfway through the intersection, the Honda leaps ahead; the driver has punched it.

By instinct I jam the accelerator to the floor, and the 'Vette shoots out too, first catching, then blowing by the Honda. I can tell he's flat out, but within a block I'm hitting eighty mph, and he's three or four car lengths back.

Knowing that there's a stop sign a few blocks ahead, I ease off the gas. I flash; maybe the guys in the Honda will be pissed that I've shown them up. But when I stop and they catch up to me, I glance over and they're all laughing. The driver toots his horn and gives me a thumbs-up sign. I wave through the smoky windows of the 'Vette.

This is the coolest thing that's ever happened to me.

After the race I realize that I don't want to go all the way into downtown Spokane. I decide I'll cruise over to the Northtown Mall.

My adrenaline's still through the roof from my race with the Honda, but I try to calm down and take it slow and easy as I drive down Rowan Street. I look at the speedometer: thirty-seven mph. Not bad for a thirty-five mph zone, but I tap the brake to be totally legal.

That's when I see her, an incredibly gorgeous girl in tight blue jeans and an Old Navy sweatshirt, standing by the side of a gold SUV with its emergency flashers blinking. She doesn't try to wave me down, but she obviously needs help. I think that she looks a lot like Becka Thorson, a legendary goddess-cheerleader at my school. She's *really* cute—she looks *exactly* like Becka.

I pull over.

She hurries over to the 'Vette, and I lower the passenger side window.

She smiles and says, "Wow, driving this thing, I thought you'd be some old dude."

I laugh.

She laughs too. "Sorry, it's a beautiful car; it's just that normally kids can't afford these things."

I don't say anything.

She laughs again. "Am I being rude enough? Let's start over. Hey, nice car, thanks for stopping."

"Hey, you're welcome. What's wrong with your Pathfinder?"

"I don't know. It just died suddenly, right along here. All I could do was coast to the side of the road."

I ask, "Did it seem like a gas or an electrical problem?"

I've been listening to Don carry on about the 'Vette for a couple weeks now—I know the lingo.

She gets a funny, hopeful look on her face. "Are you, like, one of those auto shop guys who know all about cars?"

"Not really. I know some stuff, though. Let's take a look."

She says, "Thanks."

I park, and we start walking toward her rig. She asks, "I know you, right? You go to Thompson?"

I'm shocked that she knows I even exist, but I pull it together enough to say, "Yeah, I'm Jordan James, and you're Becka Thorson."

She smiles. How can she be surprised that I recognize her? She's one of our school's most popular girls, a cheerleader, and THE most gorgeous human being in the history of the world. We are both eleventh graders, but I've never had any classes with her, and we went to different middle schools, so she probably doesn't know anything about what happened to me—about my dad, I mean.

She smiles. "Jordan, yeah. . . . Sorry, I've seen you around, but not very often."

I smile too. "Yeah, I get that a lot."

She says, "No, really, I remember you from last year, seeing you then. Where have you been?"

I don't want to say, In zombie land, so I blurt out, "I've been out of the country for a while."

"Really, where?" she asks.

Damn . . . I'm such an idiot. "Oh, all over, Paris, Berlin . . ."

Paris? Berlin? What the hell am I saying?!

She looks skeptical but lets it drop as we reach her Pathfinder.

"I think I know what's wrong," I say after trying to start the Pathfinder and hearing it turn over and over.

"Really?" she asks. "Can you fix it?"

"I think so. Have you got a dollar?"

She looks confused.

I say, "You see this gauge here on your dashboard, the one that says Fuel? When that little arrow goes below empty, like it is right now—that's a sign that you need some gasoline. These things run wayyy better with gas in them."

"Oh, my God!" she says, laughing. "Are you kidding me? I'm just outa gas?"

"Yep."

"Sheesh!" she says, and laughs some more.

By the time we get back with a half gallon of gas (Becka holding it carefully, thank God, so that none spills onto the floor of the 'Vette), and I pour it into the Pathfinder, she's told me all kinds of things I already knew about her, and two things that I didn't know: that she doesn't, "at the present time," have a boyfriend, and that she loves "cool cars."

All I've said about myself is my name and that completely stupid crap about having been out of the country. What was I thinking? Out of the country? Right, like Mr. International Jet-setter? I also mentioned that I'm not dating anyone "right now" either. I don't actually say I own the Stingray, but she's assumed it's mine, and I don't deny it.

Becka writes her name and phone number down on a scrap of paper she pulls out of her purse.

"Call me!" she says as I get back into the 'Vette. "I wanna go for another ride in your car."

I smile and say, "I'll call."

I think, MY car, huh? How the hell am I going to pull this off?

Wally asked me what could make the risk of stealing the 'Vette worthwhile. Wait till I tell him about Becka!

EIGHT

The good news is that I get the car back and make it to my house and no one is the wiser. The bad news is that I've met the most gorgeous girl in the world, and she thinks I'm this real cool guy because I *own* a Stingray.

Lying on my bed at home, I dig into my pocket and find the slip of paper on which Becka has written her name and phone number. I study her handwriting and try to sniff the ink, which is bright pink. I say her name about ten million times. "Becka Thorson, Becka Thorson, Becka Thorson . . ." I touch the writing, rubbing the scrap of paper, reading the message over and over. Becka Thorson, 555–7778, Becka Thorson, 555–7778.

In other words, this girl has turned me retarded.

At some point I flip the piece of paper over and see what's on the other side. It's a recent receipt for pool chemicals: five gallons of chlorine and some stuff called pH reducer. In the corner it says that the chemicals are for "Thorson gas-heated pool, 20,000 gallons, 1123 W. Indian Canyon Road."

So what am I facing here? Becka Thorson drives an almost-brand-new Nissan Pathfinder, and she lives in one of the swankier neighborhoods in Spokane. She has a swimming pool—hell, she has *everything*! Her life is perfect.

Perfect, perfect, perfect—she's going to be thrilled to find out that not only do I *not* own a Corvette, but that I'm a lying sack of shit ("I've been out of the country") and that I'm half an orphan.

I look at her handwriting again: Becka Thorson, 555–7778. And again. Becka Thorson 555–7778, Becka Thorson, Becka . . .

I grab the phone and call Wally. I tell him about meeting Becka.

"Yeah, right," he says, laughing.

"Really, Wally, it's true."

Dragging out the words like he's talking to a lying four-year-old, Wally demands, "*You* met Becka Thorson . . . *the* Becka Thorson? *You* met her and she *likes* you?"

"I swear to God."

Wally laughs again. "She loved the car, right?"

"Yeah."

"Your 'Vette."

I get quiet.

"Yeah," Wally says. "This is gonna work out real good for you."

As usual, Wally, in his own demented way, is probably right; I'm screwed.

When Mom gets home from work tonight, I'm still super high about meeting Becka. The hell with Wally and all his negativism—Becka liked me, I could tell.

Mom comes through the front door, and I holler out, "Yo, Mommy-o!"

She laughs and answers, "Well, hi, J-boy."

These are nicknames from like a thousand years ago, back when Dad was still alive and we were this big, happy family. Or at least we thought we were.

"Why are you so festive?" Mom asks.

"Sorry," I answer.

Mom laughs again and says, "You know I didn't mean it like that. I'm just glad to hear you sound so full of beans."

"Full of beans?" I tease her. "That's really hip, Mom; no, really, you are one cool mack mommy, so in touch with the youth—"

Before I can finish, Mom, a fake anger in her tone,

says, "That's it, smart aleck! Yer getting smacked down . . . smacked down hard . . . *now*!!!"

Like I mentioned before, Mom's got a good straight right; she has a good left hook, too. I'm outa here! If I can reach my room before she catches me, I'll be saved. . . .

NINE

The next day at school, Wally and I sit together in second period, Current World Problems. He can't wait to ask me more about Becka. She's such a somebody at our school, and we're such nobodies.

Wally, still straining to believe the whole thing, asks, "Are you actually going to phone her?"

"Yeah."

"When?"

"Soon, probably tonight."

"Are you going to tell her the truth?"

I've foolishly admitted to Wally my dumb-ass "man of international intrigue" horseshit. I consider his question for a second. "If we actually go out, I'll tell her the truth, face-to-face. Not on the phone before we even see each other again."

Wally ponders this for about a second. "Yeah," he

says, "that's a good idea—you should actually be with her when she dumps you."

"Thanks, Wal."

Don and I are working on the 'Vette in his driveway when I bring up the nitro for about the hundredth time.

Don looks at me. "You sure got a hard-on about this nitrous booster, don't you?"

I say, "Sorry if I'm bugging you. . . ."

"No." Don laughs. "It's fine. I haven't even tried the nitrous myself yet. Nitrous is not a toy. It causes incredible strain and can make a car old before its time—nitrous is the methamphetamine of the internal combustion engine."

I ask, "So why have it?"

"So that this bad girl, admittedly mild by classic Corvette standards, won't just look good but can deliver if the demand ever arrives."

I flash back to my drag race with the guys in the Honda, the rush of beating them and of them appreciating and respecting the 'Vette. "I know what you mean."

"Oh yeah?" Don asks, looking at me kind of funny.

I stutter, "I mean, I get what you're saying."

Don nods.

TEN

"Hi, is Becka there, please?"

"I'm sorry, Becka's been called away on a matter of national security. She's been arrested and—"

I hear a loud grunt and a muffled, brief struggle.

"Hello!"

I recognize her voice right away, having played it over in my head maybe ten billion times since we met.

"Hi, Becka, it's Jordan, the Corvette guy—"

Her laughter interrupts me. "I know who you are. How you doin'?"

I ask, "National security?"

She asks, "Do you have any little brothers or sisters?"

"No."

"You're so lucky, you have no idea—they're so cute when your mom first brings them home, but then they start walking and talking and learning to answer the phone."

I laugh.

Becka, in a voice so sweet that I feel almost dizzy, says, "But enough about my tragic plight. How are you and how's the 'Vette?"

I'm ready for this. "I'm good, great really, but the 'Vette's in the shop."

"Bummer," Becka says. "When do you get it back?"

"Uhhh . . . I'm not sure really. . . . Maybe a week."

"Geez," Becka says. "What's wrong with it?"

I have an entire explanation that involves motor mounts and valve covers and the alternator—suddenly it all sounds like way too much, so I just say, again, "I'm not really sure."

Becka laughs. "Does it appear to be a gas or an electrical problem?"

At first I think she's serious, but now I remember that I asked her the same thing that first night we met.

I laugh. "You think maybe I might be out of gas?"

"I don't know—stranger things have happened."

I love this, I love her voice, her sense of humor; *Becka Thorson* is kidding around with *me*! It seems impossible.

Finally I suck it up and spit out the reason for my call. "I was wondering if you'd like to go out."

"Stop it!" Becka snaps.

I stutter, "Ex-excuse me?"

Becka quickly says, "Not you," then pulls her mouth away from the phone and yells, "Billy, you're *such* a dead man!"

I hear a boy's laughter in the background.

Becka says to me, quickly, "Call me later in the week; I'll be able to talk better after I've finished hiding my brother's body. I can drive if your 'Vette isn't ready—you drive the next time. By the way, did you know that nobody at school even knows you have a Corvette?"

Surprised, I ask, "What?"

"Yeah," she says, obviously a little distracted, probably planning her brother's murder. "Don't you ever drive it to school?"

I stammer, managing to mumble, "I . . . uh . . . no, it's not insured for daily driving."

I'm not sure if this even makes any sense, so I change the subject. "How do you know about me at school?"

She laughs. "I have my sources, although I have to admit you're a bit of a mystery—most kids don't know you."

I ask, "Is that right?" Then, quickly, "You still want to go out, though?"

Her final words as she hangs up are "Call me tomorrow."

I can't believe my luck.

I phone Wally, because I've promised him I'll keep him up to speed on the Becka situation.

I say, "She told me to call her back."

Wally says, "Good, that's a good sign."

I laugh. Trying to be funny, I say, "You really think so?"

Wally, sounding totally serious, says, "Well, it means she probably doesn't know what a lying piece of shit you are yet."

Wally definitely has a special gift for buzz kills. I say, "I suppose that's true, Wally."

"You better tell her, right away, about the car."

"Yeah, I know."

"You better tell her soon."

I feel worse and worse the more we talk.

I say, "Yeah, I'll do that, Wal. Listen, I gotta go."

Wally says, "Just one more thing."

"What?"

"Before she dumps you, will you ask her if any of her cheerleader pals need a boyfriend?"

In as nasty, sarcastic a voice as I can manage, I

answer, "Sure, Wally, no problem—I'll pimp you up big-time."

Wally, totally not even noticing my tone or maybe just ignoring it, says, "Thanks, man!"

When I phone Becka tonight, we have a longer visit. It's cool getting to know her better. She comes from a pretty big family, five kids all together. Her youngest sister, who is four years old, has Down syndrome, which doesn't seem to bother Becka. In fact, Becka shares a bedroom with her. Becka's the oldest kid in her family. She's also a gymnast and a cheerleader-goddess. She's a National Merit Scholar and incredibly beautiful. In other words, Becka Thorson is perfect.

"But can you cook?" I ask her, trying to be funny.

"Not a thing." She laughs. "I've burned water! Nope, prepare to spend the rest of whatever meager income you ever earn after 'Vette repairs on Caesar salads for moi."

I hesitate a second.

She laughs. "Don't worry, big boy, that wasn't a marriage proposal."

Actually, marriage doesn't sound like such a bad plan; that's how totally gone I already am on her. I'll never, ever meet a girl as cool as Becka again. We agree that our first date will be a walk in Riverside State Park followed by frozen yogurt.

"How's the 'Vette?" she asks, smashing my marital fantasies to smithereens. It's the car she's hot for, not me; remember that, you idiot.

"Still in the shop," I answer—hey, I'll take her any way I can get her.

"Do they know what's wrong with it yet?"

"Uh, not really. So you can drive us this Friday?"

Becka says, "Sure, I'll pick you up around six."

I give her my address and hope like hell that Don won't be home that evening working on my . . . I mean . . . *his* Stingray in his driveway!

ELEVEN

Mom is hopeless at advising me about my date. Not that I've asked for or want any advice, but she has lots of it to offer anyway—all worse than useless.

"Girls like to be treated special," Mom tells me, like this is some big breakthrough in gender relations.

"Yeah, I got that. Thanks, Oprah." I don't mean to sound like such a smart-ass, but Mom's been sitting on the edge of my bed for the whole time I've been trying on different shirts and trying to get my hair right. I can't handle another suggestion.

Mom starts, "If she asks about—"

I interrupt, "Mom, that's it. I can't listen to this—will you *please* just leave it alone. It's not like this is the first date I've ever had!"

Actually, it *is* the first date I've ever had, other than meeting up with girls at school dances in the seventh grade. Were those really dates?

Mom knows that since Dad died I've kind of gone into a shell. Hell, "kind of"? The average garden snail sees more action than I have. She's tried to help me but failed miserably, since I won't let her.

Mom and I went to grief counseling for quite a while, and that seemed to help *her* some, but nothing has helped me. I know lots of kids whose parents have gotten divorced. Some of them lose contact with their dads. But having your dad *die*, especially the way my dad died, and knowing that you'll *never* see him again, is different from having him just move out. I don't know how else to explain it.

Mom starts to say, "When your dad and I—"

Even before she sees my expression, she catches herself. "Sorry, honey." She knows better than to mention Dad to me. We made an agreement at the end of our counseling sessions that I didn't have to talk about Dad until I'm ready. Mom's been really cool about honoring this; I know it's made her nuts sometimes, wanting to help me, wanting to make it better; I mean, she's a nurse, for crying out loud; it's her *job* to help people! But she respects that I don't want to talk about Dad; she knows that I can't . . . that I *won't* talk about him.

She says, again, "Sorry."

I look away from her and say, "Never mind. Anyway, I'm good here—can I have a little privacy?"

I slip on my gray SPOKANE CORVETTE CLUB T-shirt that Don gave me. "Okay," Mom says, "I'll let you finish getting ready."

She starts to head for my bedroom door but pauses and turns back. "Don asked me to go out for dinner and a movie again tomorrow evening—you still doing okay with that?"

I laugh at her. "Of course. I'm the kid, Mom—you're the adult."

"Yeah, Jordan, I know that—every time I write a check for the mortgage, pay the bills, and bring home groceries, I recall that little fact."

I say, "Sorry. Of course I'm fine with you guys going out. I hope you crazy kids have a groovy, wacky time."

"Smart-ass," Mom says, but she's smiling.

In my head I've gone through my *plan* for this first date with Becka about a thousand times. We'll walk in the park, and I'll overwhelm her with my wit and charm (or at least I'll avoid saying anything too stupid). I'll ask her lots of questions about herself and show her how interested I am in her, proving that I'm not some typical guy with a one-track mind (even though I'll probably be thinking the whole time about what she looks like naked—yeah, one-track mind). We'll have some frozen yogurt at TCBY and I'll pick some exotic flavor so she'll know I'm cool (like that'll do it). Then it'll be getting dark and maybe she'll want to park someplace, maybe down at Arlington Park, where kids go to make out. We'll get hot and passionate and she'll fall madly in love with me, and when I'm sure she can handle the truth, I'll say, "There's something I have to tell you. . . ." I'll admit to being a social nobody who's been at school the whole time, just invisible and worthless, and I'll tell her the truth about the 'Vette. Maybe the shock of my not owning the car will be offset by the fact that I've got the guts to steal it—girls love that outlaw, bad-boy stuff.

Six o'clock has come and gone. In fact, six twenty has also come and gone. I sit on our couch in the living room trying, unsuccessfully, not to stare out at Northridge Road like the obsessed, *stood-up* geek that I am. The only things going right are that Mom is smart enough to leave me alone and Don and the 'Vette are out of sight.

I phone Wally. "Becka isn't coming."

"Did you actually think she *would*?" he asks, laughing, like he's known all along how crazy I was. He says, "Maybe you hallucinated the whole thing. Or maybe she's just been playing you—you know, acting nice, but probably she's really like that psycho woman in *Fatal Attraction*. You don't own a pet rabbit, do you?"

I glance at the clock on the living-room wall: six forty-five.

I say, "She's probably busted me. She's probably on the phone with her cheerleader pals right now, laughing about the dork in the 'Vette T-shirt who's actually a nobody and who doesn't own a Stingray and who's sitting on his couch like an idiot, just staring out at an empty street!"

Wally, suddenly sounding very worried, asks, "You didn't mention me to her, did you?"

I say, "I thought you wanted me to."

Wally laughs cruelly. "Not once she's on to you. . . . How stupid do I look?"

I'm considering my answer to his question when, stunned, shocked, and then *totally* juiced, I see Becka's gold Pathfinder cruising slowly down the street toward my house.

I yell at Wally, "She's here."

Wally asks, "Where?"

"On Northridge, right here, right now!"

Wally quickly starts, "Ask her about the cheerleaders, tell her about me, ask her if—"

I interrupt. "I gotta go!"

"Ask her!" I hear Wally yelling, "We're in, man! We're cool! Listen, ask her about—"

"I gotta go, Wal, I'll ask, I promise."

"We're in, man!" I hear Wally screaming; then, "Be sure and smile at her once in a while—"

I hang up.

TWELVE

Not until I open the passenger door to climb in do I notice Becka's sister Lori, the Down syndrome four-year-old, sitting in a car seat in the back.

"Sorry," Becka says. "That's why I'm so late. My mom had to go out and my dad was supposed to be home early but he couldn't get away from work. He didn't even call until after six. I'm really sorry!"

I force a smile. "No, it's cool." I look back at Lori. She's little and blond and cute.

"Hi, Lori, I'm Jordan."

She smiles and makes a happy gurgling noise that sounds a little bit like "hi."

Obviously, my date with Becka isn't coming off quite as planned. The main missing ingredient is the groping I've fantasized. I didn't expect to score, but it would have been nice to get a little physical. That's obviously not gonna happen.

After we go to the park and take our walk, Lori scrambling all over the place and Becka taking my hand in hers as we go along one of the flat trails out near Seven Mile, we go to TCBY for frozen yogurt. I end up with chocolate and M&Ms topping, not exactly the exotic cuisine I'd planned on ordering.

It's a nice night, so we sit outside at one of the white plastic tables. A tiny percentage of Lori's dessert, strawberry frozen yogurt with sprinkles, served in a waffle cone, actually makes it into her mouth. Most of it smears all over her face. But she's a sweet enough little kid; I don't really mind having her along.

I still need to come clean with Becka and tell her the truth about myself. Maybe with her sister here, she'll be looser. I figure I have a bit of an advantage, being so nice and noncomplaining about Lori being with us, so after some small talk, without any decent diplomatic setup at all, I just spit out, "I've actually been around since the ninth grade. I wasn't really out of the country."

"I know," Becka says.

"I'm sorry I lied to you, but I've never been to

Paris. I've been around forever."

Becka looks serious. "I know."

A little surprised, I ask, "How did you find out?"

"I told you, I have my sources."

I can't tell if she's mad or waiting for me to say more, but I just shut up.

Finally Becka asks, "Why'd you lie to me?"

I'm ready for this. "I was afraid you might not give me a chance if you knew that I was just some invisible geek."

She smiles.

I have my next lines all ready, my admission that the 'Vette isn't really mine. I take a deep breath and am ready to tell her the truth when Becka laughs and says, "Well, an invisible geek with a 'Vette is different than an invisible geek without one, right? It's a good thing you own that Stingray."

I force a smile.

But then Becka says, "Just don't lie to me again, all right? I *really* hate lies!" She pauses a second, and then smiles and says, "Berlin?"

My face turns bright red and I say, "I know . . . sorry."

She grabs a napkin and reaches over and wipes some of the mess off of Lori's chin.

I can't tell for sure what Becka's thinking about me, but in another few seconds she looks up and smiles.

I think I'm all right.

THIRTEEN

Don can tell something is bothering me.

"What's going on?" he asks as we polish the chrome wheels, front and back, on the driver's side of the 'Vette. We're getting ready for the coming weekend's Show and Shine. Don works on the front wheel and I take the back.

Obviously I can't tell Don my specific problem, that my girlfriend—well, not exactly "girlfriend," but the girl I'm going crazy over—believes that his 'Vette belongs to me and that the only reason she's giving me the time of day is for "my" car.

So I talk in general terms. "This girl I like thinks I'm somebody different than I really am."

Don asks, "Like James Bond or something?"

When I don't laugh, he says, "Sorry. I'm not that great with 'relationships.'" He pauses, blushes, and adds,

"Well, thanks to your mom, I'm getting a *little* better."
He asks, "You like this girl a lot?"

"Oh, yeah. She's perfect."

Noticing the way I'm working with the metal polish on the chrome beauty ring, Don says, "Let that stuff stay on there a little longer before you wipe it off, Jordan; give it time to do its thing."

I look at the chrome on his wheel, and then back at mine; his is far shinier.

"Okay," I say.

Don asks, "This girl, you say she thinks you're somebody different than you really are. I'm guessing you either lied or let her believe some stuff that wasn't true."

"Both, really."

"Can you tell her the truth?"

I say, "I did tell her part of the truth, but she said that if I was lying any more, she wouldn't like it much . . . and there was one part I couldn't admit to. She doesn't like being lied to."

Don smiles. "Yeah, unlike the rest of us who get such a big kick out of it." Then he says, "Seriously, though, when I want to tell somebody the truth, I know it's easier if it feels safe to do it—but at some point, safe or not, you gotta just take the risk of being honest."

I think about that. "Yeah, maybe so."

Don glances at my chrome wheel and says, "See how much better that looks?"

I nod, but I'm thinking about the phrase Don just used. "The risk of being honest."

I don't even know where to start with Becka—the car would be only the beginning. I can't tell her about my dad— I mean, I don't talk to *anybody* about that. What good would it do anyway, except to convince her that I'm a total loser, from a total loser family?

Monday morning at school walking to our first classes, Wally is slightly more direct. "You're screwed," he says.

"Yeah, I know."

"I mean totally screwed."

"Yeah," I say, annoyed. "I should have told her."

Wally, without missing a beat, asks, "Did you ask her about . . ." But catching my killer glare, he shuts up.

"I'm screwed," I say.

Wally says, "Is there an echo in here?"

Don's invited me to go with him to a local Show and Shine, a car show where he's taking the 'Vette. There are dozens of these kinds of shows around Spokane, matching the dozens of car clubs in town: classic

Mustangs, classic Fords, classic Chevys, any number of hot-rod groups. There are two major Corvette clubs in Spokane, and Don's joined both of them. I decided it might be kind of cool to go.

I've never gone to a car show before, and Don has taken the 'Vette to only a couple. We're driving up Cedar Road, toward the top of the hill to the Five Mile Grange, where the show is being held.

I glance over at the dashboard and pretend to just notice that the speedometer is working.

"You fixed the speedo."

"Yep," Don says. I can tell that he's almost as nervous as I am about showing the car.

"So what happens at this show thing?" I ask. "Is it a competition, like with awards and stuff?"

"Yeah," Don answers, "but a small one—probably just a few dozen cars."

As we turn the corner onto Strong Road, I remember the first time I ever rode in the 'Vette, along this very stretch at 110 mph. That seems like a long time ago. During the weeks since then, so much has happened: the car, Becka, Don and my mom (they've had, like, half a dozen more dates), Don and me . . . things are changing faster now than they have in a long time . . . in the last three years anyway, for sure. I know that I'm feeling better: I'm even starting to listen a little in some of my classes at school. My life doesn't totally suck now—I'm not sure what to think about that, so I try not to think about it at all. I mean, before, I had nothing . . . I *was* nothing . . . so what was there left to lose? Now, it's like . . . well . . . like I just said, I try not to think about it.

The closer we get to the grange, the more cars I see. There are classics of every make and era, and lots of cars I don't even recognize: hot rods, customized so that you can't even tell what they once were.

We pull up to a sign that reads ENTRIES AND REGISTRATION, and Don checks us in.

He asks the lady at the registration table, "Where do you want me to park?"

She points across Strong Road to the old redbrick schoolhouse. "The restoration classes are over there, in front of the school. Just find any place. Class winners are announced at three, and all ballots are due back as soon as you fill 'em out, no later than two-thirty."

She hands Don his ballot, with a listing of all the cars in the show arranged by class.

Don smiles and says thanks, and idles slowly over to the lawn in front of the school.

He explains to me about the ballot. "Judging of cars

is done by the participants. We look at one another's cars and pick what we think are the nicest rigs in the various classes—best restoration, best modified, best classic; the categories are all listed right here. Course, I don't have to worry about that today."

"Why's that?"

Don smiles. "Because today you're going to judge."

"Me?" I hesitate. "I don't know anything about these cars."

"Sure you do. You know that our 'Vette's the prettiest rig here, right?"

I laugh and look around. "There're *a lot* of pretty cars here, Don."

He smiles. "See, you're already judging. Most guys at small shows like this don't know much more than we do, and it's all for fun anyway. I'll show you what to do."

We've been at the show for about half an hour and I'm trying to do a fair and good job at being a car judge. I'm looking closely at the Modified Pick-Ups and Sport-Utility Vehicles when I feel a tap on my shoulder. I turn around, assuming Don will be standing there since he's the only person that I know here.

"Hi," Becka says, smiling.

My first reaction is to smile back and to feel a rush of excitement at getting to see her.

She asks, "What're you doing here?"

Before I know what I'm going to say, I blurt out, "Showing the 'Vette."

Now comes my second reaction—pure panic!

Becka beams. "The Corvette's here? It's finally back from the shop?"

The impossibility of my situation hits me. I begin to stutter and mumble, "Yeah, um, it's here . . . I . . . um . . ."

"Where?" Becka asks excitedly, looking all around. She's got two kids with her. I'm thinking they're her brothers.

"You brought your brothers along," I say, trying stupidly to change the subject, stalling for time.

"Where's the Corvette?" Becka asks again.

"Yeah," one of the boys adds.

I'm trapped. How can I explain Don to Becka, Becka to Don? What if she says something about riding in the car? About its being mine? What if she says anything about . . . anything? A rush of hopelessness and despair crashes through my gut. I'm *so* screwed!

"Well?" Becka insists.

I have to answer her. "We're over in the In-Progress Restoration group."

"Where's that?" Becka asks.

I point across the street to the front of the school.

Becka looks over and spots the car. She also sees Don, sitting in a folding chair next to it.

"Is that your dad?" Becka asks.

"My dad's dead."

"What?" she says, her face surprised and a little shocked.

"He died when I was thirteen."

"God," Becka says softly, touching my arm. "I'm sorry, I didn't know."

"It's no big deal. He was a jerk anyway. And I don't talk about him. . . ."

Becka gives me an even stranger look when I say this, but she touches my arm again and squeezes it a little.

I don't know what else to say, so I nod back toward the Corvette and Don. "That's Don Lugar, a neighbor guy. Kind of a grumpy character, but I needed him to enter the show."

"Why?" Becka asks.

"You have to be eighteen or older." I'm not even sure if this is true, but I haven't see any other guys my age with cars here.

"So you had him enter for you?"

"Yeah," I answer, sinking deeper and deeper in the quicksand of my lies. "Like I said, he's kind of unfriendly, but I needed him to help me, to pretend the car's his so that I could enter the show. He has to act like it's his rig."

I'm amazed at how easily these lies unfold and feed off one another, growing with each second, with every word.

Becka doesn't say anything for a while, then asks, "Can we go look at your car?"

I answer quickly. "I can't now. I'm judging, and I've gotta finish."

I think for a second about encouraging Becka not to go over to the 'Vette at all, but I can tell already that her little brothers will never allow that. If Becka says something to Don about riding in the car, I'm dead. I'll have to take my chances. Becka and I chat back and forth for a few more seconds; I can't help but notice how incredibly beautiful she is.

I glance back at the Corvette and, as if by some kind of miracle, Don is gone! I look all around the area where the car is parked, and he's nowhere in sight. Maybe he's using the restroom? Maybe he's gone to the refreshment stand? Wherever he is, he isn't near the 'Vette right now!

"You guys should go over and look at the car right

away!" I encourage them, a little too aggressively.

"We could wait until you're free," Becka suggests again.

But the younger of her two brothers whines, "I'm tired. Let's go now!"

Becka looks at me, exasperated.

I quickly say, "No, you guys go ahead. I'm gonna be a while finishing this."

The whiny kid says, "Come onnnn. . . ."

Becka smiles at me and squeezes my arm again. "Sorry, but the brat rules can only be stretched so far."

I smile back.

As they walk across the street in the direction of the Corvette, she looks back at me and smiles. "Call me."

There's still no sign of Don.

"I will," I answer, wondering whether my luck will hold long enough for her to ever want to talk to me again.

I beat it around the far side of the grange building, out of sight of the Corvette, where they can't see me. I hide among the Modified/Customs, specifically near a 1953 Mercury hot rod, chopped and painted deep burgundy, except for bright red and yellow flames on the fenders and hood. It's a beautiful car, and it gets my vote in its class, although, to be honest, I'm so nervous that I don't even look at any of the other cars in that group.

I kill as much time as I can. Finally, maybe half an hour later, I peek around the corner. Becka and her brothers are nowhere in sight. Don's back in his folding chair, sitting next to the Corvette.

Standing right in front of him, talking, is Wally.

What's he doing?

I told Wally last night that we were bringing the 'Vette here, but I didn't really expect him to come by.

First Becka and now Wally? At least Wally knows not to mention anything about my stealing the car.

I approach Don and Wally and say, "Hi, Wal. What're you doing here?"

Wally laughs. "Nice to see you, too, butt-munch."

Don laughs too.

Wally says, "I just came by to look at this 'Vette you've been telling me about. You're right—it is beautiful."

Don smiles and says, "Your buddy showed up about half an hour ago and asked me to look at a couple of the Mustangs with him and answer a few questions."

Wally says, "Yeah." Then he adds, "Did you know Becka Thorson was here?"

"Oh yeah?" I act surprised.

"Yeah," Wally says. "She and a couple little kids."

I say, "Her brothers."

Don says, "I thought you didn't see her."

I stutter, "I didn't, but probably . . . you know . . . little kids . . . I don't know. . . ."

I look at Don. "Did you meet her?"

"No, I was showing Wally the Mustangs."

I glance over at Wally. His expression is totally obvious, and he might as well be screaming out, "You owe me one!"

"Right," I say, half smiling.

"Yeah," Wally says. "Right."

My palms are sweaty, and my heart pounds in my chest. My throat is dry, and I feel the dampness under my arms as beads of perspiration roll down my sides. I silently promise myself that I'll never steal the 'Vette again, I'll tell Becka the truth and come clean and just be thankful that I've managed to not get busted. I swear that I'll be an honest, upright, law-abiding citizen from now on.

Wally saved my ass—how weird is that?

After Wally leaves, Don and I stick around for another hour.

The 'Vette wins a prize for second place in class.

As Don and I cruise back down the hill, he asks, "What was your favorite part of the day?"

For some reason I flash instantly to the moment when Becka squeezed my arm and the look on her face when I told her about my dad. I also think about Wally saving me; a hundred images of great cars rush through my skull, too. I look at the award that I'm holding in my lap and I feel the rumble of the 'Vette as we drive toward home.

I turn to Don. "My favorite part of the day? This, right now, just cruising."

He smiles. "Me too."

I'm feeling great. Great enough that I decide I'm going to tell Becka the truth about the 'Vette. I'm definitely going to tell her!

FOURTEEN

Becka and I are going on our second date tonight. And I'm driving the 'Vette—yeah, that's right, the 'Vette.

Nope, I didn't fess up.

It's a Wednesday, of course, and I told Becka that I can't stay out late on school nights with the car, and she bought it. It's true, both for the reasons I explained to Becka and for the other, *real* reasons that I haven't admitted yet.

I didn't want to take the car again; I wanted the lies and the fear of being caught and all of that to stop—but I can't give it up. Things are going good now; for a change I'm actually having fun.

So I'm just riding the wave.

I've gotten so good at grand theft auto that it's scary—it almost feels like I'm not even doing anything wrong.

* * *

When I get to Becka's house and pick her up, we cruise down Indian Trail Road; I ask what she wants to do.

"Let's go park at Arlington," she says.

I laugh. "What, are you getting all scandalous?"

She laughs too. "There's nothing scandalous about parking at Arlington. But of course, you're a geek, right, you wouldn't know that."

I punch the 'Vette and we roar forward for half a block. She grabs the black plastic grip on the door, just like I did that first time I felt the Stingray's power.

"Don't make me turn on the nitrous," I tease her, easing off the accelerator.

"Dang," Becka says. "This sucker goes, doesn't it?"

"She," I say.

"Excuse me?"

"She's not an it, she's my baby," I say.

"Hmmm?" Becka smiles. "Is that right? Your baby, huh? Your one and only?"

I smile but don't say anything.

Becka says, "*She's* the one who's scandalous."

"Oh, yeah," I agree.

Becka, a soft, sexy tease to her voice, says, "Get us to the park . . . and we'll talk about scandalous."

When we get there, we do more than just talk about it.

* * *

After I get back home, I phone Wally; I have to tell somebody what's happened. It's like a dream. If no one else knows, it won't even feel real.

Wally can't believe it. "She actually kissed you?"

"Yeah, we made out."

"How far did you get?"

"I'm not gonna go into details, Wal. We kissed and made out."

"Did you feel her up?"

"A little bit."

"What do you mean, a little? On top of her shirt? Under her shirt? On top of her bra? Under her bra? How far did you get?"

"No comment, Wally."

"You made out with Becka Thorson—you!!" His voice sounds like he's in a trance. "You kissed her and felt her up—"

I interrupt: "A little."

"Yeah, whatever. This is incredible. Amazing. My best friend is gonna nail a cheerleader."

"Let's not get carried away here, Wal."

But Wally, on a roll, can't stop himself, "Come on, man, this is how these things start—some kissing, some making out, and the next thing you know you're buying condoms by the jumbo pack. And she must have some cheerleader girlfriends, right? She must—"

"I gotta go, Wally."

"Yeah, okay, but just remember—"

"I got it, Wal."

"Good!"

We hang up.

God, life can be good sometimes—I wish I could just shut everything else out and concentrate on that.

When Mom gets home, I'm doing homework at the kitchen table.

"What's this?" Mom asks, smiling. "Those can't be schoolbooks, can they?"

"Of course not," I kid her back, and hold the book up for her to see: *American History: Freedom and Democracy*. "This is just a little light reading, you know; they were out of nasty magazines."

"Good boy," Mom says. "I'm proud of you. Did you have a good day?"

I blurt out, "Becka Thorson and I went out again."

"Oh, really," Mom says. "Did you have fun?"

"Oh, yeah," I answer, a little more enthusiastically than I mean to.

Mom asks, "Did she come by and pick you up?"

I say to myself, No, I drove Don's 'Vette—she loves

it; it's an aphrodisiac, better than date drugs or too much beer! But I catch myself and just lie, "Yep."

Mom says, "You can use the Honda anytime, you know?"

I say, "Thanks, Mom."

But I say to myself, the Honda . . . come on . . . not when I can get my hands on the 'Vette!

FIFTEEN

Don recently replaced the old, broken radio that was in the Corvette. He ordered a brand-new replica from Eckler's Corvette Catalog. The new radio looks just like an original; it has CORVETTE in shiny letters across the top, and the dials are old-fashioned-looking. The face of the radio looks analog, like the original radios looked, but when you turn it on, the analog dial fades and a digital face appears, complete with thirty preset stations. The system is wired for a CD player, which Don hasn't installed yet, and plays cassette tapes.

For date number three I pick Becka up at her house at six. She's waiting at the front window, and before I've even pulled the 'Vette into the driveway, she runs out to greet me, followed by her two brothers.

I say, "Hi," as she opens the passenger door and climbs in.

She leans over and kisses my cheek, and Billy, the older brother, goes, "Eeeww!"

Becka gives him a drop-dead look, which makes Brian start to tease us too. "Eeeww." Brian laughs. "Kissy-kissy little boy-boy . . ."

Becka lowers the window and says, "If any sign of intelligent life comes around, please don't say anything. They'll lose all hope."

This shuts them up long enough for us to make our escape.

"Wow!" Becka says suddenly.

"What?" I answer, looking around fast.

"You got a new radio? Or is that an old radio?"

I'm surprised she's noticed it so quickly. I explain about it being a replica. But I realize that I haven't actually tried it out yet. I could kick myself for not getting more familiar with the system before I picked her up.

"Can I turn it on?"

"Sure," I answer, hoping she won't ask me how.

She reaches for the left-side button and turns it clockwise, the same thing I'd have done.

Suddenly Elvis Presley's voice blasts out at us from all four speakers, incredibly loud. He's singing "Hound Dog," and the volume is deafening.

Becka laughs and turns the sound down just enough for me to hear her ask, "You like Elvis?"

I say, "What?"—stalling for time. The face of the stereo has the letters PLY and an arrow pointing to the right. This is a cassette. Why would I have an Elvis Presley tape playing in *my* Corvette if I didn't like him? Is the tape all Elvis or is there something even more horrible lurking just ahead? Neil Diamond, maybe, or the Partridge Family's greatest hits—who knows what Don likes? At a total loss for an explanation, I smile weakly, hoping for the best.

Becka gushes, "Elvis." Then, sounding almost embarrassed, "The King."

I can't believe that she's serious, that she actually *likes* Elvis Presley, but then she sighs and says, "Just listen to him."

She's right; I have to admit that he *does* have an amazing voice.

Becka starts tapping her foot. "My parents were Elvis junkies when they were young, way back in the 1950s and 60s. They never grew out of it, and they still play *Elvis's Golden Hits Volume 1*, which I listened to about ten billion times growing up. I know every word to every song. God, what an astonishing waste of RAM." She laughs. "Heck, I even learned to *dance* to this stuff!"

As we drive, I'm stunned by the weirdness of this scene: Here's this incredibly popular cheerleader-goddess, rocking to Elvis Presley music recorded more than thirty years before we were even born.

Becka does a really funny Elvis imitation. She isn't lying about knowing all the words, and she sings along to every song. Her best moments are when Elvis turns words like "I" into three syllables, "I . . . I . . . I . . . love you . . . won't you lovvve me?" She even sings along with the guitar solos, singing the notes they play, "Do-do-do-wah-wah-wah-do-do-do."

The song "I Want You, I Need You, I Love You" plays. Elvis sings like he's the most hungry, desperate, love-struck guy in the history of the world (man, I can relate), his voice full of passion and desperation. It's so over the top that even I like it, but hearing Becka sing along makes it all the more wild—it's both ridiculously funny and at the same time almost good. Becka actually has a great voice!

We've been out for almost an hour, just listening to the music and cruising. It's been really fun. I definitely think of Becka as my girlfriend now. How demented is that? She's so beautiful, and at Arlington Park we kissed and made out; she cares about me, she really does, I know she cares and I know—

She interrupts my fantasizing. "Did your parents love Elvis too?"

"I don't know."

"Did your dad ever—"

I interrupt. "I told you, Becka, I don't talk about him."

She looks a little hurt, but she reaches over and touches me, stroking her fingers down my face. Normally I think I'd love her doing this, but I feel really tense. I blurt out, "My dad's dead, that's all, there's no point in talking or thinking about him—what good does it do?"

Becka asks, "It was that bad, huh?"

"I don't know; I don't talk about it—okay?" Suddenly it feels like my head is going to explode.

"But Jordan, you have to talk about it someday. It's such a sad thing, it's so—"

Without planning it, I slap her hand away and scream, "Shut up!" as loud as I can. "What do you know about it?! You don't know anything!"

Becka looks shocked, but at least she stops talking.

The car is deadly quiet.

I should say something, apologize, or try to change the subject, something, *anything*, but I can't.

We're driving back toward Becka's house, and in

the total silence between us, my mind races back to that day my dad died, *that day he killed himself!*

I can see him sitting there, the gun still in his hand; I tried to get him out of the chair and down onto the floor, but he was so heavy that I kind of dropped him. His head made a loud thump when it hit the carpeted floor, and a squirt of blood oozed out of the bullet hole in his temple. He landed on his back, and I kneeled down next to him. My heart pounds in my chest now, just like it did that day. The stubble of Dad's sandpaper beard scratched at my lips as I tried to breathe life back into him; I remember the stench of death. I can see that horrible look on his face again, so calm and peaceful, and my tears ran down my cheeks and dropped onto his neck and shirt collar. My mind was racing: What will Mom say? What's going to happen? Why, Daddy? Why'd you do this? What have you done? What did I do? Is this my fault? And what did you mean, "bullshit," Dad? What's bullshit? You? Me? Everybody? Everything? Daddy . . . Dad . . . Oh, God, please help me, God. . . .

It all races back—crashing over me.

I turn into Becka's driveway, unsure of how I even drove here—it's like I'm in a trance, but I'm sweating and breathing really hard.

"I . . ." I start to speak, but Becka is already jumping out of the car. It's a good thing, 'cause I can't think of another word. I can't think of a single thing to say.

She slams the door of the 'Vette and runs into her house.

I think she's crying.

SIXTEEN

I've tried to phone Becka, but she won't talk to me. At first she had her brother Billy tell me that she wasn't home. I called back, but when she said hello, she sounded really cold.

"Hi," I said. "Listen, I'm sorry about yelling at you."

"You hit me," she says, real softly, but not nice, just low and angry.

"No, I didn't."

"You hit my hand."

"I knocked it away from my face."

"That's hitting."

"I didn't mean it like that. . . . I just meant . . ." I can't find the right words.

She says, "Hitting is hitting."

"Bullshit!" I say, then quickly, "Sorry, I just mean—"

She interrupts, "Stop calling me. Don't call me anymore!" Then she hangs up.

I feel totally numb, but at least it's a feeling that I recognize.

At my dad's funeral, Uncle Terry, Mom's brother, spoke about my dad. He said lots of nice things, stuff about how funny my dad was and how good a guy he was and how much he loved all of us and the Seattle Mariners. Uncle Terry said lots of great things about Dad, in spite of how Dad had killed himself, and gave Dad lots of compliments. But as Uncle Terry talked and as people all around us were crying and blowing their noses and trying to avoid looking over at Mom and me, I started to feel more and more numb, like novocaine was pumping through my whole body.

I feel that again now, thinking about Becka.

SEVENTEEN

I'm trying to explain to Don about what happened. "She said not to call her."

"Don't, then," Don says.

"Not at all?" I ask.

He stops looking at the oil dipstick he's checking and glances over at me. "Which part of 'don't call' didn't you get?"

I feel my ears turn red with anger.

Don notices and quickly adds, "Shit, Jordan, I'm sorry. I'm not trying to be mean. But people have to get over stuff in their own ways—and a real friend accepts that and gives a person space. After all, it sounds like you got mad at her for not giving you space, right? Now it's your turn."

I nod. What he says makes sense; I mean of course it makes sense. Still, I'd hoped that Don would say, "Call her anyway."

He asks, "This girl means a lot to you, right? I mean, you *do* care about her, don't you?"

I nod again. I haven't told Don what Becka and I fought about; I haven't told him what I did, or how horrible it was for me to think about my dad again. I haven't told *anybody* that. But my feelings remind me of how it felt after Dad died, that weird, horrible numbness. I don't want to go back there again. I don't know what to do.

Don interrupts my thoughts. "Do what she asks, Jordan; don't call her. She knows your phone number, and she'll call you when she's ready."

I say, "Okay."

But I don't mention that I feel like I felt in those days after I lost my dad, during the worst time of my whole life. I don't mention that I'd almost rather die myself than feel this numb again!

I don't tell Wally what Becka and I fought about either—he wouldn't understand it anyway.

But his brilliant suggestions are typically amazing, a little less than helpful.

He asks, "So she's super-vulnerable right now?"

"I guess."

"She must be all broken up."

"Yeah, maybe a little bit."

Without missing a beat, Wally says, "Be sure and take a condom along to go comfort her."

"What?"

"You know, just in case."

"Jesus, Wal, you're an ass. I'm not sure when or even *if* I'll ever hear from her again."

"All the more reason to be prepared," Wally insists. "Make-up sex, buddy; this might be your best and last chance."

"Wally, does the phrase 'sociopathic dickhead' have any meaning to you?"

He laughs. "Hey, I'm not the guy who lied his head off to the love of his life while stealing his mom's boyfriend's car."

One of Wally's most annoying traits is his tendency to sometimes be right.

Truthfully, Mom is the most helpful.

I explain, "She was asking about Dad, about stuff I didn't want to talk about."

Mom nods that she understands and then says, "I know how hard that is for you, sweetie. It's hard for me, too."

"You didn't see him like I—" I stop myself.

But Mom finishes my sentence for me. "You're right, Jordan, I didn't see your dad right after he died—I didn't go through what you did. You were incredibly brave that day, trying to help him."

I'm starting to feel crummy again, even talking this much about it. My hands are shaking a little bit. Mom notices and stops talking.

After a few seconds, she says, real softly, "I know that my seeing Don has brought a lot of stuff back up for us."

I say, "I like Don."

"I know you do, honey. You can like him, and it can still be hard. Let's face it; we've spent the last three years in survival mode, nothing more than that. I see it all the time at the hospital—people curling up and making every breath count, just hanging on and fighting for their lives—in a lot of ways, that's what we've had to do."

"I guess," I say, but I'm thinking about Becka and me, wondering why this had to happen *now*, when things were finally starting to get good.

Again, Mom kind of reads my mind. "When you push things down inside yourself, try to ignore pain, it never really disappears—it just hides out and waits, then it comes up again."

I kind of get what Mom's saying; I know because I

felt the same way, when I argued with Becka, that I used to feel anytime I thought about Dad killing himself, the same fear and anger followed by going all numb and stupid.

Mom says, real gentle like, "Do you think that maybe this fight with Becka is a way for you to start dealing with some of this?"

"Yeah," I say, but then I get up to leave the room. "Yeah, maybe."

I can't talk about this anymore; even though I get what Mom's saying, I just can't do this now. Not yet.

Mom says, "Whenever you want to talk, Jordan, you know that I'm here, right?"

I nod.

EIGHTEEN

Wally is at my house after school hanging out. I still haven't heard from Becka. But Wally is good at collecting school gossip.

He says, "I guess she's having a hard time—she must have really liked you or something."

"Oh yeah?" I ask.

"Yeah, she goes home every day and just hangs out with her brothers and sisters . . . they've got like ten kids in their family."

"Five."

"I heard ten."

"You heard wrong—I went out with her. She's got two brothers, Billy and Brian, and two sisters."

Wally says, "The youngest kid is all messed up."

I say, "The youngest is Lori and she's got Down syndrome. She's not messed up."

"What would you call it?" Wally asks.

He really isn't an asshole; he just acts like one sometimes.

I try to find the right words. "Developmentally . . . handicapped or delayed . . . something. I don't know, but messed up isn't right."

"Okay," Wally says. "Anyway, I guess Becka's taking your breakup pretty hard."

I feel myself getting pissed, not at Wally really, but just pissed off generally. "You think *she's* messed up," I snap at him. "What about me? She just wanted to talk about stuff that I don't talk about. She thinks like a regular person, but you don't lose a parent and have things be the same—it changes *everything*. How do you talk about that? How do you explain something like that?"

"Yeah," Wally agrees—like he'd know. His parents are still together, with Wally and his sister, Claire, who is twelve. How the hell could Wally understand what I've gone through? I almost say something but bite my tongue. It isn't Wally's fault, any more than Becka's, that the world is such a crappy, unfair place.

Suddenly, out of the blue, I ask, "You wanna go for a ride in the 'Vette?"

He looks at me like I'm crazy. "Do I want to become

an accomplice to grand theft auto? Gee, tempting . . . but . . . no, thanks."

"Suit yourself," I say.

Wally asks, "How many times do you think you can pull off that shit before you get busted?"

I answer, real smart-ass, "You didn't fill out an app."

"What?"

"When my old man died, you never applied for the vacant position."

"I'm not trying to be your dad. I'm just—"

I interrupt. "You're just saying the same *worthless shit* that he'd say to me."

Amazingly, for the first time I can remember it ever happening, something I've said actually shuts Wally up. I get quiet too. Although neither of us says it out loud, we both know that it's time to change the subject.

We eat some junk food and play video games for an hour or so, but the truth is I can hardly wait for him to leave so that I can go get the 'Vette. Becka may have dumped me. Wally may not have a clue. But when I'm behind the wheel of the Stingray, nothing seems to hurt anymore—everything feels okay.

NINETEEN

Almost two weeks have passed since Becka and I broke up. I haven't tried to call her again, and she sure hasn't called me.

Wally says, "You blew it, buddy."

"How did I blow it?"

"You shoulda nailed her when you had the chance."

"When did I ever have a chance?"

"Yeah," Wally admits, "I suppose. But you were so close—we both were."

Wally is watching his one chance to move from Invisibility Street in Loser Land to the swanky neighborhood of Big Shot Boulevard in Cheerleader Heaven disappear.

"Sorry, Wal."

"Yeah," he says, and pauses. "At least now you

can stop stealing Don's car."

I don't say anything.

What I'm not saying to Wally, what I'm not saying to anybody, is that somewhere between Becka and the Corvette I stopped feeling numb, stopped wanting to hide out and just be invisible. Yeah, my dad is dead and that's *messed up*. But there's more to life than being a goddamned frozen, freakin' zombie. Somewhere, somehow, and some way, I've thawed out. And now it's like I'm starving for everything I've missed these last three years.

Becka has been a part of this, but she's gone now—which leaves me just one lady: the one with the NOS sticker on her ass.

I'd decided not to take the 'Vette again unless I absolutely had to, but losing Becka has made me feel so bad that I've been worried that I'll get stupid again. I have barely talked to anybody for the last few days, right up till about five seconds ago, when I heard Adam Scott bragging about his classic GTO.

"I can kick anybody's ass in this town," Adam says to a few starstruck freshmen in the cafeteria at school.

I laugh, and he hears me.

"What?" he asks.

"Nothing."

"That's what you drive, right . . . *nothing*?"

The freshmen laugh, too.

"I've got a ride."

"Yeah, right," Adam snarls.

Adam isn't a tough guy, at least not a fighter or bully. He *is* a motorhead, and his red 1965 "goat" is beautiful and, within the world of our school, a legendary car.

But I can't let the freshmen laugh at me, so I say, "I borrow a friend's 'Vette once in a while."

"Bullshit!" Adam says. "What kind of 'Vette? What year?"

"A '76 Stingray."

Adam laughs, "A '76, huh? A gutless wonder? What's that pull, a hundred and eighty horses?"

He's right about factory horsepower for 'Vettes in '76. From the showroom, with their original crappy catalytic converters, Stingrays were rated at 180. But in Don's car, with her rebuilt engine, her tweaked exhaust system, not to mention the nitrous package, we can crank 380 hp.

Before I can explain that to Adam, he laughs again.

"Even if you did have a seventy-six 'Vette, it doesn't belong in this conversation."

"It'd beat your goat," I say, having no idea if this is even close to true but feeling too defensive of the Stingray to let Adam talk about her in that way.

"Right!" Adam says, and laughs. "Name the time and place."

I should hesitate; at least, I should think it over, but instead I hear myself blurt out, "The stadium, tonight, six o'clock." Thank God it's a Wednesday!

Adam looks me straight in the eyes and says, as serious as a heart attack, "You got it."

The freshmen are impressed, but then again, they're only frosh.

For the rest of the afternoon at school, among the motorhead population especially but a lot of other kids, too, the race is *the* big news of the day. "The stadium" is Joe Albi, on the northwest side of town, only a few miles from my neighborhood. Kids have drag raced there for years. The huge parking lot surrounding the stadium has half a dozen long, straight stretches of blacktop, some of it crumbling and cruddy but most of it fairly smooth. Every kid in town knows that Albi is the place to race.

Wally catches up with me by our lockers at the end of the day. "You're gonna race Adam Scott?" he asks.

"Yeah."

"Do you have a will?"

"Don't be stupid."

"Are you crazy?" Wally smirks.

Suddenly I spot Becka leaving the building at the other end of the hallway. "Wally, shut up," I say, and watch Becka go out the door.

Wally follows where I'm looking.

With Becka out of sight, Wally starts up again. "Listen, I know this thing with Becka is hard on you, but there's no need to commit suicide. What the hell do you think you're doing? Shit, man, they'll throw your ass *under* the jail if you get caught."

"How am I going to get caught? I'm careful."

Wally laughs. "Yeah. Right. Mr. Careful!"

"Whatever," I say.

Wally shakes his head. "Does the phrase 'next of kin' mean anything to you?"

I ignore his question and ask, "You gonna come watch?"

"Of course," Wally says. "Like I said, they'll need somebody to identify your body—it's me or dental records."

"Shut up!" I say again, but I start to feel a little nervous.

Still, nervous is better than numb.

I've known since Don explained about the nitrous booster that I'll have to try it someday and that I'll probably get killed doing it. Not really *killed*, maybe, but the thought of controlling the 'Vette with 200 extra horsepower scares me; it just doesn't seem that there's any safe way to do it.

I turn on the nitrous and lift the red cover over the activator switch and click it on, too. I can't hear anything change in the sound of the car over the engine's loud rumble, or feel anything different, but then I wouldn't; the nitrous is filling the lines but won't kick in until I slam the gas pedal all the way to the floor. This will happen in a few seconds—when the 1965 GTO next to me, and "my" 'Vette, get the signal to go. I can hear Adam's big engine, 400 cubic inches and 400 horsepower, revving over and over again. He's ready.

But so am I.

It's six ten. We're idling, side by side, a dozen feet apart, on the longest straight stretch of asphalt at Joe Albi Stadium. Our engines rev up over and over. The roadway runs close to an eighth of a mile long.

Adam, having noticed the small red-and-black Edelbrock NOS sticker in the back window of the 'Vette, says, "You didn't say you had nitrous."

It's a fair point. "I know, sorry, I should have said something."

Adam says, "No, it's good. You wouldn't have stood a chance without it. This makes it more interesting."

"Yeah," I say.

He also notices the larger sticker in the middle of the back window of the 'Vette, one I bought as a present for Don and insisted that he put up. Adam, reading it, says, "'Does not play well with others,' huh?" These are the words written over a pair of angry red eyes. I wonder if Adam can make out the smaller print below: "It seems others don't like to lose."

He smiles. "Doesn't play nice, huh?"

I might be blushing, but I don't say anything.

Adam says, "You ready?"

I nod; my throat feels too tight to talk.

It's like a hot-rod movie. A girl from school stands between us, right in front. I don't like her being there; what if one of us gets sideways and hits her? But this is the way it's done.

She raises her arm over her head and raises one

finger, another, and as she raises a third finger, she drops her arm.

Scared that I might hit her, I don't floor it right away. Adam does; his goat is a four-speed manual, and he pops his clutch. My slower start doesn't hurt me too much, as Adam's rear wheels break loose and smoke pours off of them. We're past the starter girl in only half a second, and then I floor the 'Vette, too. Adam's tires grab in the same moment as my nitrous kicks in.

The rush from the nitrous is amazing. The 'Vette's always felt fast, always *been* fast, but it seems a hundred times faster now. My head slams back against the head-rest and is stuck there; I can't pull it forward if I want to. The torque makes my eyes water. The vibration in the steering wheel is stronger than I've ever felt it before. The front wheels lift up off the ground as the car feels ready to explode. Instead she flat-out flies.

Adam's GTO is right next to me. I may have inched ahead of him slightly, but I can't tell for sure. The nose of the Stingray protrudes so far out that it's impossible to tell where I am in comparison to the goat. Glancing over, I see that Adam and I are right next to each other. There's hardly any back and forth as our cars charge forward with incredible power. In a matter of only seconds, we're running out of room. I back off.

Adam lets up a moment later. We slow down together.

The crowd of kids watching is standing back at the starting line, and I can hear them cheering as Adam pulls up next to me and stops.

He rolls his window down, and I lower my passenger window so that I can hear what he's saying.

"Good run, Jordan, I think you got me."

I say, "Thanks, but I don't know, I'd call it pretty even."

Adam smiles and says, "I can live with that. Shit, that NOS really kicks, doesn't it?"

"Yeah."

"Gonna have to get me some of that," Adam says.

I say, "Well, don't look for me out here if you're running nitrous on top of four hundred horsepower."

Adam laughs. "What do you mean, don't look for you? Friends don't let friends win races in Chevy shit." He laughs again.

I smile back but don't say a word. I'm thinking about what Don told me about the damage nitrous can do to the 'Vette's engine. I hope everything is all right.

Adam says, "We better get out of here before the cops show up."

I nod, and he takes off.

Wally reaches me before anyone else, having run all the way from the starting line. His eyes are about the size of pie plates. He yells, "That was pretty amazing!"

"Thanks," I answer.

"You better get out of here."

I say, "Yeah, I'm gone."

"The race," as it was called, is all the rage at school for a couple days, longer among the motorheads. But even at the height of my newfound fame, I have bigger things on my mind.

I start taking the 'Vette more often, even on nights when I know that Don is in town but out, like when he and my mom are on a date.

I know it's totally lame to justify it in this way, totally self-serving and a wimpy excuse, like I'm blaming Becka for it, but I think what's happening with her is part of the reason I'm getting more and more out of control with the 'Vette.

I've found a route, a drive that's perfect—my own personal test track.

Waikiki Road is mostly straight at the beginning,

with only a few wide, easy curves, heading westbound, along the Spokane Country Club. This straight stretch ends in a ninety-degree right turn away from the entrance to St. George's, a rich kids' private school.

But the next part of the road, a little over a quarter of a mile, is free of any entry roads and all but one or two driveways, and leads down to a small bridge over the Little Spokane River. I can get the 'Vette up to a hundred mph along there, no sweat, and still have time to ease off for the tight set of S curves up a small hill, where Waikiki Road turns into Rutter Parkway. Once through those curves, the road straightens out again, and for three or four miles it varies between long straight stretches and wicked-sharp curves. There's hardly ever any traffic and I've never seen any cops, so I can concentrate on putting the 'Vette through her paces.

It's about seven miles out, and then I turn around and retrace the same route back home. If I don't hang a U-ey, Rutter turns into Indian Trail Road, which leads straight by Becka's house. I *almost* always turn around before I get that far, because when I drive past Becka's, it feels creepy, like I'm some stalker geek.

The more I drive the route, the more comfortable I am with it. And the more comfortable I am, the more risks I take. Maybe "risk" isn't the right word. I'm not really driving dangerously. But I'm pushing my speeds up, in the straight stretches and in the curves.

I'm getting totally hooked on the rush.

TWENTY

The phone rings, and I pick it up and say, "Hello."

"Hi."

It's Becka.

I try to keep my voice calm, "Hi. . . . How you doin'?" Of course I'm really excited that she's finally called, but I'm also kind of nervous; I don't want to blow this by getting weird on her again.

"I've been swamped!" she answers, and her tone of voice sounds relaxed and almost happy. "Between cheerleader practices, National Merit garbage, and classes, I've been staying really busy."

"Yeah, I know what you mean," I say, really stupid because I have no idea what she means—I'm obviously not a cheerleader and I have about as much chance of being in the National Honor Society as I do of . . . I can't even think of anything more unlikely.

Becka doesn't seem to notice, though. "It's crazy,

for sure," she says, then hesitates and says, "I've missed you."

"Me too."

"What have you been up to?" she asks.

I don't want to sound like the lunatic I've actually been, so I just tell her, "I've found this incredible drive, out by the Little Spokane River and the country club. I call it 'the route,' and it's really fun."

"I'll bet," Becka says. "Why don't you come over and pick me up and show me?"

Her timing couldn't be better. It's a Friday night, and Mom and Don are out to dinner and a movie. Don's driving his Pontiac, and they won't be home till at least ten. I can easily go grab the 'Vette.

"Sure," I say. "I'll be there in ten minutes."

"I'll be ready," Becka says. Then she adds, kind of cautiously, "After the drive, maybe we can talk."

Of course, I know what she means; she probably wants to know more about my dad. But it's cool. If I can get back with Becka, I'm willing to try anything. Besides, I think I'm finally ready.

On the drive over to Becka's going via the route, I drive a little more conservatively than normal. I want to show off to Becka how great the drive can be, and I'm saving the car for that. I actually obey the speed limit most of the way, only standing on it after the St. George's turn, on the straight stretch that leads down over the little bridge. Along there I push the pedal to the floor and hit about ninety-five mph before I notice a red pickup truck up ahead, starting to ease out of a driveway. I hit my brakes, and the driver of the red truck sees me and stops abruptly. As I roar past him, still going seventy in the thirty-five zone, I hear his horn blasting at me. I hit the S curves into Rutter Parkway and, once at the top, check my rearview mirror to make sure the truck isn't following me. Once I see that I'm in the clear, I take it easy the rest of the way to Becka's.

It feels great having Becka sitting next to me in the Corvette again. I've missed her. She grabs my arm and squeezes. "You're looking handsome."

"Yes, I am," I say, and laugh.

Becka teases me. "Of course, behind the wheel of a car like this, even really old guys look okay."

I smile, thinking about how happy Don always looks when I see him driving the Stingray, Mom riding shotgun. For half a second, for some reason, I think about my dad, too, but I push him out of my mind. I turn back to Becka and just smile.

We cruise to the end of Indian Trail Road where it

makes a long, gentle right-hand curve and becomes Rutter Parkway: the route.

The 'Vette is warm, all her gauges in the proper ranges, gas tank half full. We're ready.

"You got your seat belt on?" I ask, although I already know that she does.

"Is this it?" she asks nervously.

"Yep."

She says, "Take it a little bit easy, okay?"

She knows how excited I am to show off.

I look at her and smile. "I promise I'll be careful, really; you can trust me."

"I know," Becka says.

Instead of slamming down the gas, I ease the pedal forward and our speed increases gradually. I don't want Becka to be too scared; she needs time to adjust. We hit eighty-five mph pretty quickly and I ease off.

"You okay?" I ask.

Becka smiles. "That was fun!"

"Good."

I push the accelerator down again, a little bit harder this time. We hit ninety-five before I back off.

"Damn." Becka laughs. "This thing really hauls."

As we approach the first set of curves, I'm ready. I know the road perfectly. These turns have a fifteen mph speed limit—I've taken them at forty mph, but I slow to thirty for Becka's first run-through.

As we fly through the curves, Becka laughs and screams and lifts her arms up over her head, like a little kid on a roller coaster. I glance at her for half a second; her mouth is wide open, head back and eyes shut tight.

We move into another short straight stretch and then into and out of another curve—I hit the gas, and we shoot up to seventy mph. The 'Vette is handling it perfectly. At the bottom of another curve is another straight stretch. We're hitting eighty-five before I ease off for the next set of sharp turns.

Suddenly I see headlights ahead, so I ease off a bit more. But we're still going over seventy mph as we fly past a county sheriff's car. I glance in my rearview and see his brake lights flash. There's a small turnout only a few yards up from where he is; I see him spinning around to come after us.

"Uh-oh," Becka says. "Wasn't that a cop?"

I don't say anything, but I slam the accelerator to the floor. We're just coming out of a curve, and for the first time ever, the 'Vette fishtails but quickly straightens out as we power forward.

"What're you doing?" Becka yells.

"I'm gonna lose him."

"No!" she says. "Don't."

"Don't worry," I say.

"Don't do it, Jordan," she says, scared.

As we accelerate through the next set of curves, she stops talking. We both do.

I catch glimpses of the cop car behind us. He manages to get reasonably close through the curves. But as soon as I reach back and turn on the nitrous, then hit the activator switch and floor it, he doesn't have a chance. Although I'm concentrating on the road, I glance down and see speedometer needle bouncing back and forth between 135 and 140.

Once we're off the route, with the cop nowhere in sight, I take a crummy dirt road over the prairie back to Becka's house.

She's quiet all the way, pale, her hands kind of shaking.

Just before we get to her place, suddenly she screams, "That was stupid!"

Startled, I say, "What?" although I know exactly what she means.

"Don't act dumb! Outrunning a cop! Why would you do such a crazy thing? You could have killed us!"

I flash on telling her everything, the whole truth

right now: This car isn't really mine, in fact it's stolen; Don isn't really a grump, he's my mom's boyfriend and a friend to me, too, who I'm totally screwing over; my dad, well, my dad . . .

It's all too much, but I try to start. "I . . . this car . . ." I stutter.

But the second we stop in her driveway, Becka jumps out and yells, "You are *such* a jerk! All you care about is this car!"

I get a little mad myself now and say, "You wouldn't even *talk* to me if I didn't have this car."

"What?!" Becka yells.

"You said so yourself—a geek with a 'Vette isn't the same as a geek without one!"

"God, you thought I meant that? Do you actually think I care more about a stupid car than about you?"

"I—" I try again, but Becka interrupts, "You're an idiot!" and slams the door in my face.

I almost yell, "Don't take it out on the car," but I manage to just shut up.

I'll explain everything later, the next time we talk, after she's had a chance to calm down. That is, if she'll ever speak to me again.

I drive home the same way I drove to Becka's, on the same terrible, rutted back road over the prairie. The cops won't be looking for me up here. I ease along, driving slowly up the crummy road, a street I would *never* take the 'Vette on unless I had to.

Finally I'm at the top of Northridge Road. No cops anywhere in sight. I say to myself, I made it.

As I idle toward Don's driveway, I think, This has *got* to stop. That was just too close. I've got to knock this shit off!

I'm thinking that exact thought; I really am, even *before* I spot the two Spokane County sheriff's cars parked in front of Don's house.

TWENTY-ONE

There are times when you know you're just screwed, the jig's up, there's no way to escape your life. It's like when you're out driving, having a horrible day, and you see a sign that says NO RIGHT TURN, and you say to yourself, That's for sure, sometimes there's no right *anything*! You have no chance, nothing except reality is left, and it totally sucks.

It felt like that when Dad killed himself.

And it feels a little bit like that again right now.

I could easily spin the 'Vette around, do a quick 180-degree turn and take off again, but what's the point? I feel a tiny bit like I felt three years ago, when I heard that gunshot—hopeless and trapped.

I ease the Corvette into Don's driveway; the three cops, two men and one woman, stand on the front porch. This is the first time I've seen cops and cop cars in our neighborhood since the night Dad killed him-self. From Don's porch they look at me, and one of them puts his hand on his gun, not like he's going to draw it and shoot me, more like he's just resting his hand there; still, it bugs me. I slow the 'Vette down even more; by habit, I push the garage-door opener.

The other man cop, not the one touching the gun, yells, "Stop right there!"

Startled by the loudness of his voice, I hit the brake pedal too hard, and even though I'm going really slow, the 'Vette jerks to a sudden stop. The cop who yelled yells again. "Get out of the vehicle and keep your hands where we can see them!"

As I open the door of the Corvette and get out of the car, the lady cop and one of the men step to the side and I notice, for the first time since I pulled up, that Don is standing there on the porch with them.

Don and one of the cops, the one with his hand on his gun, stand there staring at me. The lady cop and the other cop get in one of the police cars and leave together. I get out of the car and walk over to Don.

I want to say something to him, want to apologize at least, but I can't talk, I can't think of the right words; I feel ashamed and sad. I don't care what they do to me; whatever it is, I deserve it. The cop car reminds me once again of how it felt when Dad killed himself, the embarrassment and shock and humiliation—and the fear.

I'm thinking about this when Don suddenly asks me, "What'd I tell you about the rules when you were *borrowing* the Corvette?"

I stare at him, thinking that I've misunderstood. "Sorry?"

"You heard me, Jordan—I told you *never* to speed when you borrow the 'Vette, and you know it. Then, on top of it, you run from the police!"

"I—" I start to speak, but Don interrupts.

"This is Jack Davis. He's my wife's brother."

"I . . ." I start again but stop myself. What the hell is happening? Why aren't I under arrest? What difference does it make what the cop's name is? How come Don's acting crazy? I think of all these things, but all I manage to spit out is "You don't have a wife."

Don says, "My ex-wife. And that's not the point. Did you or did you not run from the police out on Waikiki Road twenty minutes ago?"

I hesitate, thinking, Shouldn't I have an attorney here? Shouldn't my mom, at least, be here? But instead I answer, "I was out there and I was speeding. . . ." I hesitate again, and in an instant I decide to tell one last lie. "But I didn't know that was a cop behind me—"

Don interrupts again. "A policeman?"

I say, "Sorry, yeah, a policeman, I didn't know it was a policeman."

This seems like the smartest thing to say, and if I'm reading Don right, it's what he wants me to say.

Don turns to Officer Davis. "You didn't turn on your pursuit lights?"

The cop, a huge guy with a big belly and thinning hair, smiles at Don. "I wasn't a hundred percent sure it wasn't *you* in the car." He turns to me and says, "For future reference, if we see your license plate, you might as well hand us your home address. And LUV'NNOS is kind of a tough plate to miss."

Don says, "You're lucky, Jordan."

The cop pulls out his ticket book and looks at Don. "You sure you want me to do this?"

Don says, "Absolutely. He broke the law."

The cop turns to me, asks for my driver's license, and says, "I'm going to write you a citation for going sixty in a thirty-five-miles-per-hour zone. Frankly, I know you were going a little bit faster than sixty; I hit one fifteen before you left me in the dust, but anything more than thirty miles over the limit is Reckless Driving; I'm gonna give you a break."

He fills out the ticket, I sign it, and he snaps his book closed.

Don says to me, "We'll talk about this tomorrow, first thing in the morning. Go home."

I can't believe my ears; I just stand here and stare.

"Go," Don says, and turns and starts talking to the cop.

I start walking across Don's yard toward my house, still confused. Don's a good guy, but this doesn't even make sense. I get most of the way to the street, then stop and look back. "I'm sorry, Don. I'm really sorry, I—"

He interrupts. "We'll talk about it tomorrow, first thing." He turns his back to me.

When I walk in the front door to my house, I tiptoe through the hallway toward my bedroom.

Mom yells out from her room, "Hi, honey."

I freeze in my tracks. Her voice sounds sleepy and relaxed. I yell back, "Hi."

She asks, "Were you out with Wally?"

She doesn't know anything about me taking the 'Vette. I answer, "No, with Becka."

"Oh," Mom says. I can hear her happiness for me in her tone. "That's great. I'm glad you two made up.

Did you have a nice time?"

I say, "I'll tell you about it in the morning, okay?
I'm tired."

"Okay, sweetie," Mom says. "Good night."

"Good night."

I go into my room and close the door behind me.

TWENTY-TWO

I go to bed, and I have one of those weird dreams that seem totally real. Not the whole dream, but the first part of it.

In the dream my dad and I are over in Seattle at the last Mariners game we ever went to together, the summer before he died. Of course, back when this happened in real life, I didn't know it would be our last time going to a game.

In the dream everything is happening exactly like it really happened that day—the sky is blue, with just a few wisps of clouds, the grass is so bright green that it seems almost blinding, and the game is really exciting. The Ms are playing the dreaded Yankees, and it's the bottom of the seventh, two outs with the Mariners trailing by one run.

As the game has gone on, it's gotten more and

more exciting. My dad, who was a die-hard Mariners fan, has been getting more and more into it. Anyway, it's a 3-and-2 count on the Mariners hitter, and the tying run is on third base. The Yankee pitcher delivers a fastball that looks way outside, but the umpire yells, "Steeee-rike!" Inning over. My dad jumps up from his seat like he's just been hit by a jolt of electricity and yells really loud, "Bullshit!"

In another couple seconds the entire crowd is booing at the ump, but in that moment before the loud booing starts, *everybody* in Safeco Field can hear my dad's "Bullshit!" boom out. I look up at my dad, and he glances down at me, and then he sits down really fast. His face is red at first, but the next thing he turns kind of pale. I can tell that he's really embarrassed about swearing in front of all these people. A minute or two later, while the crowd is still booing their heads off, Dad turns to me and says, just loud enough for me to hear, "You ready to go?"

I'm more of a football fan than baseball anyway. Dad's the baseball fanatic. Lots of times we leave games early and listen to the end on the radio so that we can beat the traffic, but there's definitely something else going on this time—does Dad know that this is the last live ball game he'll ever see? Is he afraid that somebody's gonna come yell at him for cursing so loud at the ump? Whatever. The next thing I know, we're moving down the aisle, then up the stairs to leave.

In real life this is exactly what happened, just like I'm describing it.

But in my dream things are different, things gets really weird. In the dream, right after Dad yells, "Bullshit!" a big guy sitting right in front of us—and when I say big I mean mostly fat, but also tall and kind of huge looking, almost like a giant—anyway, in the dream this guy, wearing a faded, beat-up Mariners cap, turns around and looks at my dad. There's a tense moment of silence between them, and then the giant yells, "Right on!!" and raises his hand in the high-five gesture. My dad high-fives the guy, and then they both yell, "Bullshit!" together.

Softly at first, but then really loud, all across the stadium, every voice starts yelling, "Bullshit! Bullshit! Bullshit! . . ." as loud as they can, over and over. The next thing I know, I'm standing with everybody else, and I'm yelling it too. I look at my dad and he looks back at me and he's laughing, and we're both yelling, "Bullshit!" over and over again—together.

I'm yelling so hard, and feeling so happy, that I wake myself up, still laughing in my bed!

But in another few seconds I'm fully awake. It's really early, still dark outside. Don said he wanted to see me first thing, but I don't think he had the middle of the night in mind.

Now I lie here thinking about everything—tossing and turning and never sleeping for more than a few minutes, mostly remembering my bullshit dream.

It's 5:42 A.M. I close my eyes and pull my blankets over my head, but it's hopeless; I can't sleep.

I can't stop thinking about Don. Why would he protect me when I've screwed him over so bad? It makes me sick to think about it. I've been such a jerk. I feel horrible, not because I got caught, but because now Don knows what a selfish ass I've been. That bothers me—a lot!

At 6:30 I get up. I know it's too early, but lying here trying to sleep is making me crazy. I want to get this over with.

I leave the house quietly so that I won't wake up Mom.

I ring Don's doorbell. After a few seconds he answers. He's wearing black sweatpants and a gray SPOKANE CORVETTE CLUB T-shirt, like the one he gave to me and I wore on my first date with Becka. I feel another rush of guilt, but I'm more embarrassed than anything else; my palms are sweaty and my heart pounds—my stomach is doing backflips.

Don's holding a cup of coffee, and his hair is kind of pushed up to one side, like he's just gotten up.

He says, "When I said first thing in the morning, I didn't mean this early."

"I'm sorry. I can come back later."

"No," Don says, "it's all right. Come on in."

In all the time we've spent together over these last weeks, I've never actually been inside Don's house before. We've always worked in his garage or driveway.

I follow him through his entryway and into a living room–dining room area. He has nice things: A big dining room lies straight ahead, and to the left a living room with a large couch and a couple stuffed chairs. There's a nice rug, the expensive Persian type, in the middle of the living room under a big glass-topped coffee table. The most striking part of the place is ceiling-to-floor windows and the panoramic view, from Mount Spokane on the north to the skyline of Spokane to the south.

"Nice view," I say.

"Yeah," Don answers, like he's heard it before.

He sits in a stuffed chair, and I sit on the couch.

After a few seconds of awkward silence, I say, "Thanks for covering for me."

Don doesn't say anything.

I hesitate and then add, "I don't know why you did it, but thanks, and I'm sorry, Don. It was a shitty thing to steal your car. I mean it, I'm really sorry."

Don laughs, not a big stupid laugh, more of a chuckle. It surprises me.

"What's so funny?" I ask.

Don, still smiling, says, "I was just thinking of the look on your face when you pulled into the driveway last night."

I try to smile, but I don't see a lot of humor.

Don adds, "You were *so* busted!"

I frown and ask, "Why'd you help me?"

He pauses, sips his coffee, and finally says, "Your mom told me about your dad before I even met you. I'm sorry about your father."

He's never said a single word about my dad until this moment. But it's okay—for some reason I'm glad that he knows.

Don says, "Terrible things happen in life sometimes—things we can't control. Good things happen, too, but really *bad* things sometimes. When your dad killed himself—your mom told me how you tried to save him."

I stare down at the floor and say, "Yeah, I guess—I did CPR, but it didn't help."

Don asks, "How many kids, how many thirteen-year-old kids, would have the guts to do what you did?"

I say, "It was stupid. It didn't do any good!"

Don's quiet a second. "You've been thinking you're some kind of a loser because of what happened with your dad. You've been thinking there was something wrong with you. *Losing* someone means you've *lost* someone, *period*—that's *all* it means! It doesn't make you a loser. What you don't get is that you were a hero that day, Jordan. You're still a hero in my book."

I blush and say, "What's this got to do with me stealing your car?"

Don smiles, not a big grin or anything, just a slight smile. "You've been through some horrible stuff. Let's just say you've probably earned the right to a break or two in your life."

We're quiet for a while, like the way we are sometimes when working on the 'Vette or just out for a ride, relaxed, not needing to say anything.

Don finally says, "Besides, I like your mom a lot, Jordan; she's a great woman. How would she feel if I sent you to the slammer?"

I have to smile at this one too.

Don says, "I'm not sure what the future holds for

us, her and me, all of us—but I like you, too. You're a friend, and I'm really glad you and your mom are in my life."

I don't know what to say, but I feel the same way. Finally I mutter, "I like you, too, Don—even more than just because you didn't have me arrested."

I know this sounds stupid, but Don smiles and nods.

We're silent again for a while.

I suddenly remember back to one time my dad and I were riding into town and I'd said something about coincidences and Dad had laughed and said, "There are no coincidences." I didn't know what he meant back then, but suddenly some of the things Dad used to say are starting to make sense to me. I don't know if that's a bad or a good thing.

I ask Don, "Did you know I was stealing the car?"

He looks kind of pissed off for the first time since we started talking. "How many times have you taken it out?"

I answer honestly, "About half a dozen . . . no, a few more than that, maybe more, maybe eight or nine times, usually on Wednesday nights when you were out of town."

Don stares at me. "If I'd known about it, I'd have

stopped you. I'd have had to. I gotta admit, though, when I was a kid I might have had a little trouble resisting the temptation too."

He looks me in the eyes and says, "If you thought you could get rid of me just by stealing my car, sorry, but it won't be that easy."

I feel my face go red. I look at him and think about everything that's happened since we met. I say, "No, that wasn't it; I just . . ." I don't know how to say what I'm feeling. Tears come to my eyes, but I force myself to control my emotions. "Taking the car wasn't about getting rid of you. . . . Ever since my dad died, right up until I met you and rode in the 'Vette that first time, things had been pretty bad. But since we met you, Mom and me, since then, it's been a lot better. . . . I've never . . ." I pause and take a deep breath, "I mean, both Mom and I . . . My mom really likes you, Don. . . ." I can't find the right words, so finally I give up trying.

But Don gets what I'm saying. He says, "I like your mom too, Jordan. I hope that's okay with you. Sometimes in life we get second chances—and you deserve one, not just because you're her kid, but because you're a good guy."

He pauses, like he's thinking for a few moments, then says, "You know, sometimes when you lose someone, only then do you realize how little you knew them—I mean, it's only after they're gone that you think of the million things you maybe never said. . . ."

He stops talking.

But I think about his words. Finally I say, "After Dad died, I found all these books and magazines in his desk, all these things about cool stuff and risky adventure crap like skydiving and hang gliding, stuff he'd *never* really do—it was weird, 'cause Dad never took risks at all."

Don says softly, "Everyone has his secrets, Jordan—everyone. Maybe for your dad, risks were dreams to him. I don't know, of course. I never knew him." He pauses again; then, "But I think that a huge part of loving people is simply trying to know them."

"Yeah," I agree, thinking about my dad: A million things I could have said; a million things I'll never get to say—

Don interrupts my thoughts. "Whatever your dad felt, Jordan, I have a pretty good idea how much *you* love the Corvette, so if your mom says it's all right, I'm willing to let you borrow it and drive it if you want."

I have to look at him to be sure I'm hearing him right.

Don smiles, then quickly adds, "There's a few

conditions. First off, you've got ninety days to think about what you've done, 'borrowing' the car without permission—call it probation. After ninety days, if your mom agrees, I'll let you use the car. But here's the deal: When you drive it, you have to drive carefully, and if you ever get pulled over, you stop immediately. You have to promise that you'll *never* use the nitrous unless I'm with you and I say you can. And never drink any alcohol or do any drugs when you're driving, not just the 'Vette, but *any* car—if I hear that you've been drinking and driving, that'll be the last time you use the Stingray. Fair enough?"

I don't have to think about it long. "Sure!" Then I ask, "Are you going to tell my mom about all of this?"

Don says, "No." He pauses and stares at me, then adds, "But don't you think maybe you should tell her?" He hesitates a second. "I think there's a few things you two need to talk about."

"Yeah," I say, not sure exactly what he means or why I'm feeling such a mix of good and scared feelings.

TWENTY-THREE

Mom's up and has poured her coffee. I take a deep breath and come out of my room and sit with her at the kitchen table.

"Good morning," she says.

I say, "So far, but the day is young. . . ."

This is kind of an old family joke, something she and Dad used to say to each other when they had bad news to discuss.

My tone of voice must give away that I need to talk too, because Mom looks up, staring straight into my eyes, and asks, "What's going on?"

"I have to tell you some stuff."

Mom says, "Okay."

When I'm done with explaining about stealing the 'Vette and Don saving my ass from the cops, I pause and wait for her to react.

Mom takes a sip of coffee and is quiet for a long time. When she finally speaks, she says in a low, careful voice, "Your dad was sick, Jordan."

I look away from her. This wasn't what I expected—nothing about grounding me, or how stupid I've been.

"Listen to me, honey, this has to be said *now*!" she says. "Your dad was terribly sick."

Honestly wanting to know, *needing* to know, I ask, "What does that mean? Sick how? Cancer? Lou Gehrig's disease?"

My stomach flip-flops and my hands start to shake.

Mom says quietly, "No, Jordan, not that kind of sick. Your dad was clinically depressed, and he had been for years. He'd gone off his medicine, and he was in terrible emotional pain."

"But he must have *hated* me! He killed himself when we were all alone. He *knew* I'd find him, he *knew*!"

Mom says softly, "He wasn't thinking about you or me when he did it, Jordan. It wasn't about us—it was about him needing to escape his suffering."

My chest feels real tight; I'm struggling to catch my breath.

Mom says, "Listen, Jordan, it *wasn't about us*, it wasn't about *you*! We've avoided this for a long time, and I've let us avoid it, but it's something we *have to talk about*!"

I know what she's saying—it makes total sense. It's kind of like what Don told me—things happen, both good and bad things, and we can't control them all.

Mom gets up and comes around the table and kisses my cheek and hugs me.

She sits back down and sips her coffee.

I say, "I thought that Dad must have hated me."

"I know, Jordan, but he didn't—I know he loved you."

"But he killed himself when we were here alone. He knew I'd find him, he knew that I'd—"

Suddenly, from out of nowhere, I feel this huge sob come out of me. My voice breaks, and I can't say another word. I cry and cry, burying my face in my arms as I collapse onto the kitchen table. I'm sobbing too hard to go on. My chest aches and snot pours from my nose. My throat feels incredibly tight. I want to throw up and fall to the floor and just die. I've never felt so sad, so terrible. A hundred pictures of my dad rush through my head, a thousand pictures of him: laughing, angry, quiet . . . dead. . . .

Mom comes over and pulls her chair close to mine and wraps her arms around me. More snot pours out of my nose and drips down, my face feels hot, and I can feel sweat dripping down my sides—but I can't stop crying, I can't stop, and suddenly I realize that I don't want to stop—it feels like everything horrible I've ever felt is pouring out of me. I know this sounds weird, but as bad as this feels, it feels good, too. I can't explain it—but I don't need to, words won't help me anyway—I'm crying so hard I have to fight to catch a breath.

All I can think is that it feels amazingly good to get all my tears out.

"Dad loved me," I say when I'm finally able to talk again.

"He loved us both, Jordan."

"He did, didn't he?" I say, not really asking.

"Absolutely."

"You know the last word he ever said to me?"

Mom looks at me curiously. "What?"

"He said, 'bullshit.' He said, 'It's all such bullshit.'"

Her eyes fill with tears. "I'm sure that's how it felt to him that day—lots of days he must have felt like that."

I say, "But he wasn't saying that I'm bullshit. . . . He wasn't saying that."

"No, Jordan—I promise you that he didn't mean you. He loved you."

I nod. I know deep down that what she's saying is true.

"I loved him, too," I say. "I still do."

"Me too," Mom says.

And for the next three hours Mom and I remember Dad together, not just the end, not just that last day, but everything else—sometimes we cry, more often we laugh and smile. My dad died, he killed himself because he was sick—but now he's alive again in Mom's memories and mine—he's back with us where he belongs—in our hearts; in some way I can't explain, I know that my dad is back.

Even though at the end of our talk I feel amazingly good, Mom still adds her own ninety-day sentence to Don's probation.

"You're restricted, house arrest, for the next three months."

I nod. I can handle that. Right now I could handle anything.

Mom's given me permission to take care of one final thing before my punishment begins—something

Mom knows that I have to do.

Becka hangs up on me twice before I can even get a word in.

But the third time I phone, she answers, real mad, "Stop calling me!"

I say, "I will, I promise, if you'll just let me explain."

"There's nothing you can say that makes what you did okay!"

"I know, Becka, you're right. If you'll let me talk to you for ten minutes, I promise I'll never call you again if you don't want me to."

There's a long silence; then Becka says, "Not on the phone . . . and *not* in the Corvette!"

I smile to myself. Not in the 'Vette, huh? She's got that right! I say, "I'll come by in Mom's Honda."

Becka says, still mad sounding, "I'll be waiting."

"I'm on my way."

Then Becka says, "Ten minutes."

I say, "That's all I'm asking for."

We sit in Mom's Honda at Arlington Park. I'm ready.

"The reason I ran from the cops is that the 'Vette isn't really mine. It belongs to Don Lugar, my mom's boyfriend, the guy you saw sitting next to it at the

Five Mile Show and Shine."

Becka doesn't act surprised at all. She says, "I knew the car wasn't really yours. I mean, an Elvis Presley tape? You should have seen your face. I didn't like you lying to me, but I liked you anyway."

I feel myself blush, but now Becka asks, "So your mom's boyfriend lets you borrow the car?"

"He's going to, after three months' probation is over, but that night, and the other times I was out in it, he didn't know I had it."

"So you stole it?" She sounds surprised, even shocked.

"Kind of."

"If you took it without him knowing, you were stealing it—what's 'sort of' about that?"

I try to think of how to explain everything; but suddenly I feel tired of all the lies and bullshit—there's that word again. Besides, Becka's right. "Yeah, I stole it," I admit. "He didn't know I had it, so it *was* stealing. And when I saw that cop start chasing us, I was scared. I'm sorry."

She says, "You should be sorry, you idiot." She pauses a minute to let her words sink in, then asks, "What's this probation thing?"

"Well, after ninety days, he's going to let me use

the car; I'll have his permission then. My mom's ninety days of punishment is running concurrently, since it's for the same offense."

"Wow." Becka smiles a tiny bit and says, "Sounds like somebody's been watching a little too much Court TV. This Don must be a pretty good guy."

"Yeah, he is. . . ." I hesitate a second, thinking about my next words. I'm surprised I'm going to say them, even though they feel true. "He's like a dad to me." I feel a warm shiver.

Becka smiles. "That's nice. It's neat that you have that."

But Becka isn't smiling anymore as she asks, "Why did you lie to me? I mean about the car, about everything? What could have made telling me all these lies seem like it was okay to do?"

I take a single deep breath and say, "The truth is hard for me to talk about, but I'll tell you if you still wanna hear it."

"Of course I do," Becka says. "That's what we're here for."

I take one more deep breath, and now I tell Becka the *whole* story about my dad and me, *all* of it— somehow I find the words. Mostly I talk about Dad. After all the years of *never* talking about him, it feels amazingly good saying it out loud. Becka looks stunned as I go over what happened that day Dad shot himself. She turns pale and her hands shake. Finally she cries and kisses my cheek and touches my face gently. It feels *really* nice.

For a long time after I'm done talking, she's quiet, cuddling next to me, just holding me tight—almost as tightly as I'm holding her.

After closer to two hours than ten minutes, we finally leave the park and drive the route, slow and easy through the turns and along the straight stretches. Even in the Honda it's kind of fun.

Becka says, "Did you really think I cared that much about your car?"

"Sort of."

She laughs. "You don't know much about girls, do you?"

I blush. "Well, I'm learning a little about *you*."

"But you didn't know that owning the Corvette wouldn't matter to me?"

I think about this for a second. "It mattered to me," I say.

Becka smiles, even laughs a little, and then says, "Ninety days isn't that long, you know." She kisses my cheek. "I can wait." Then she adds, pretty sarcastically, "Guys and cars . . . good lord!"

I'm tempted to remind her that the 'Vette isn't just any car, but what's the point? Instead, I smile too.

AFTERWORD

On the phone Wally says, "So they nailed you, huh?"

I answer, "Ninety days is going to pass pretty fast. Truthfully, Mom won't be all that strict about my house arrest. After all, I have a long history of putting myself in 'restriction' already."

"That's true," Wally says, but I can hear the disappointment in his voice. I haven't mentioned to him a bit of news I think he'll appreciate.

Wally says, "Well, I have to admit that it's gonna be kind of boring not having your crazy shit to worry about."

"Yeah," I answer. "Sorry about that."

There's a long silence. I can barely keep from laughing.

"Well, hang in there, Jordan."

"I will, thanks, Wal. . . . Oh, and by the way, I

forgot to mention that Becka talked about you to Steffi Turner."

"*What?*" Wally gasps.

I laugh.

Steffi Turner is a sophomore cheerleader, sweet, no boyfriend, and best of all she has long, gorgeous red hair.

Wally is stunned. "Are you serious? Are you kidding? I . . . you . . ."

I laugh again. "She's expecting you to call. She *wants* you to, she's in the phone book under Turner, her dad's first name is Carl, they live on Jefferson, and—"

"I gotta go!" Wally blurts out and then tries not very successfully to control himself, "Thanks, Jordan. . . . I mean it, man—you're—you're the . . . Steffi Turner! I gotta go!"

He hangs up.

I go back into Dad's office at our house. It's been three years and seven months since I was in here.

Mom cleared out a lot of Dad's belongings. She got rid of his books on accounting and most of his personal stuff. I'm surprised that so many of Dad's things are gone, but not too surprised. After all, this isn't his space anymore. It's just a room now, almost empty and never used—but just a room.

And still here, a little dusty after all these years, is Dad's oak desk. It looks smaller now, not as huge as it always seemed when I was little.

Has Mom gone through this, too?

I pull open the big drawer on the lower right side. I see the old papers and manila folders. I carefully lift them out of the way, and sure enough, I find Dad's secret collection of risky dreams.

I reach down and scoop up every one of the old magazines and books and riffle through them until I find the one about Corvettes. I carry it carefully, like found treasure, upstairs to my bedroom.

I find a place on my bookshelf, in front of some of my old comics and little-kid picture books that I never look at anymore. I put *Sports Car Color History, Corvette 1968–1982* so that it faces out into the room. You can't miss it; the cover is a photograph of a bright-yellow 1970 LT1 Shark and a Silver '82 Collector's Edition C3.

I don't know, and I guess I'll never know, exactly what Dad's books and magazines meant to him.

But I know what *this* one means to me: that no matter how horrible things are, somehow, if you survive, life can get better. I wish my dad had known that—I'm glad that I do.

ACKNOWLEDGMENTS

First off, thanks to George Nicholson and Paul Rodeen, my agent and his former sidekick, who helped shape this story, and to everyone else at Sterling Lord Literistic, Inc., who put up with my constant phone calls and whining.

Thanks to Toni Markiet, whose efforts at editing this book were typically brilliant and who deserves much of the credit for this. Also thanks to everyone else at HarperCollins, especially Phoebe Yeh and Catherine Onder.

I'd like to acknowledge all the usual suspects, of course—many friends and professional colleagues. Chris Crutcher, Terry Davis, Mikey Gurian, Ed Averett, Laurie Halse Anderson, Bill Egger, and my other partners in crime who live and die by twisting and turning words around. Kelly Milner-Halls for being both a writer friend and a great help with my web page. Thanks to Terry Pratt for working as my events coordinator and webmaster for a while. Thanks, Stacie, too—even though I can't ever seem to find you anymore. LOL.

Thanks to Wally and Kathy Egger, both for still liking us after we missed our flight to Europe and also to Wally for referring me to John Colliver at John's Auto Repair in Clayton, Washington, who helped me get the right info about GTOs and nitrous oxide. Also to the guys at Five Mile Auto in Spokane and to Jim Driggers of Camp Lithia and my friends at the Spokane Corvette Club for invaluable Corvette info.

Thanks to my terrific family—my sons Jesse and Sheehan,

my wife Patti, my sister Cindy, and Garren—and to my many other friends, both in the writing world and out of it. Finally, as always, thank you to my readers: the teachers, librarians, reading specialists, and young adults without whose continued support and interest in my work it would be impossible to continue finding homes for my stories.

TT

October 2005